"I couldn't possibly deprive you of your bed," he continued,

"and I'm sure that I'm right to assume you weren't offering to share it with me?"

"I most certainly wasn't!" Eden snapped back.

Marcus laughed derisively. "Blushing, Miss Moore? How delightfully old-fashioned. Yet I should have thought a woman like you would be well past that."

"I doubt you know the first thing about a 'woman like me.' Oh, perhaps you think you have all the answers, but you could be surprised to discover how wrong you are."

Jennifer Taylor was born in Liverpool, England, and still lives in the northwest, several miles outside of the city. Books have always been a passion of hers, so it seemed natural to choose a library career—a wise decision as the library was where she met her husband, Bill. Twenty years and two children later they are still happily married and she is still working in the library, with the added bonus that she has discovered how challenging and enjoyable writing romantic fiction can be!

Books by Jennifer Taylor

HARLEQUIN ROMANCE
3142—LOVESPELL

HARLEQUIN PRESENTS
1326—A MAGICAL TOUCH
1349—TENDER PURSUIT

Tides of Love
Jennifer Taylor

Harlequin Books

TORONTO • NEW YORK • LONDON
AMSTERDAM • PARIS • SYDNEY • HAMBURG
STOCKHOLM • ATHENS • TOKYO • MILAN
MADRID • WARSAW • BUDAPEST • AUCKLAND

ISBN 0-373-17274-5

TIDES OF LOVE

First North American Publication 1996.

CHAPTER ONE

EDEN had no idea who the man was. The knock on the door had startled her because she'd not been expecting anyone to call on a night like this when the waves were pounding against the rocks below and the wind was screaming like an animal in pain. She had gone to the door and opened it without pausing to consider the wisdom of doing so. Now to find the stranger standing there studying her so coldly made her suddenly wary.

'Yes?'

'Eden Moore?' His voice was low and deep yet strong enough to carry easily above the fury of the early summer storm. When Eden nodded, bewildered that he should know her name, he continued harshly, 'Well, thank heavens for that! I've been traipsing around here for hours trying to find this damned cottage!'

He made it sound like her fault and she stiffened in an instinctive response to being unjustly blamed. 'What do you want?' she demanded shortly.

'To talk to you, obviously, but I can't do that standing out here in the middle of this gale.' He pushed the door, taking Eden by surprise so that he was inside before she could attempt to stop him. He looked round, his gaze skimming over the small room which served as both living and dining area before coming back to rest on her startled face with more than a hint of cold amusement.

'I must confess that I expected a somewhat different setting for a woman like you.'

Eden stared at him for a blank moment, trying to make sense of what he meant before hastily curtailing the attempt. 'Get out! How dare you push your way in here? Get out at once!'

She flung the door wide open, holding grimly on to it when a gust of wind threatened to rip it from her hand. Fear was uncoiling in her stomach but she'd learned to harness it, turn it into anger, and that stood her in good stead now. 'Did you hear me? I told you to leave!'

The man stepped forward and calmly took the door from her, slamming it against the storm. 'I heard. But I shall go when I am ready to, Miss Moore, and not before.'

Eden drew herself up yet even though she was tall for a woman—five feet nine in her stocking feet—she still had to look up at him. 'If you don't get out of here this very instant then I...'

'You will do what?' His narrow lips quirked into a mere travesty of a smile as his eyes swept her angry face. His eyes were dark grey, cold and assessing as they lingered on her. They held a biting contempt she couldn't understand, a dislike she would have needed to be blind not to see, yet seeing it didn't help her understand.

'Just what will you do? You don't have a telephone and the nearest house is—what?—oh, at least three miles away. So how do you intend to *make* me leave?'

God, how she hated men like him, cold, arrogant bullies who thought they could dictate terms! She walked past him to the closed kitchen door, her hand resting on the latch as she glanced back. 'You're right, I don't have any of those but I do have something far more effective.'

Opening the door, Eden whistled softly, hearing the click of nails as the dog instantly obeyed and came across the tiled floor. He stopped in the doorway, his eyes going immediately to the stranger while a low warning growl came from his throat.

Eden stroked her hand over his silky head, smiling tightly at the man. 'You see, I don't need any protection apart from Drac. Beautiful, isn't he? Pure-bred German Shepherd, three years old and highly trained. If I give him the command then I have no doubt that *he* can persuade you to leave.' She paused deliberately, watching the man's face. 'Perhaps I should explain how he got his name? Smile, Drac. Show the gentleman your teeth.'

The dog bared his teeth, the huge pointed fangs gleaming in the light from the oil-lamp. Eden gave him a rewarding pat then glanced at the man again but he was exhibiting none of the usual signs of alarm. Most people presented with Drac on first acquaintance displayed nervousness, but he seemed almost amused!

'Drac as short for Dracula, I imagine?' He laughed softly, as though appreciating the joke. 'He's a beautiful beast, Miss Moore, but rest assured that you won't need to show off his prowess tonight. I didn't come here to threaten you, at least not in any physical way.'

He glanced round, taking no notice of the dog's ominous growl as he walked to the fire and spread his hands before the blaze. Eden watched him in silence, the bewilderment she'd initially felt growing stronger. Just who was he? She had never seen him before, she was certain. She would have remembered him all right, would have found it difficult to forget that coldly handsome face with its square jaw, the hint of a dimple oddly not managing to soften it, the black hair which was brushed straight back from a broad forehead, that aura of power which surrounded him. He was wearing city clothes— an expensive dark suit under a black trench coat which must have provided little protection against the raw

weather—yet somehow he managed not to look out of
place. He was a man certain of his own ability to make
things go the way he wanted them to, and he frightened
her!

Her fear communicated to the dog and his growl
became more threatening. The man glanced round, unperturbed, at ease, and Eden felt her temper suddenly
surge to life and wipe away the fear.

'Who are you?' she demanded, tossing the heavy
weight of nut-brown hair over her shoulders. It reached
her waist, thick and straight and glossy. Usually she wore
it pinned up but she'd been getting ready for bed when
the knock had come at the door. Now, as the man's cold
grey gaze slid over her, she felt conscious of her appearance in a way she hadn't been in ages.

She ran a smoothing hand down the navy wool sweater
she was wearing with faded jeans then felt annoyed that
she should react at all. 'Well?'

'My name is Marcus Cole, if that means anything to
you?'

Eden shrugged. 'It doesn't.'

'No? Well, I'm sure the name Rob Lewis does. I believe you and he are...old friends?'

There was an insulting emphasis on the last words
which made his meaning unmistakable and Eden stared
coldly at him. 'For your information, it doesn't mean a
thing! And frankly, Mr Cole, I don't like your tone!'

'And frankly, Miss Moore, I don't give a damn
whether you like it or not!' He felt in his coat pocket
and pulled out an envelope, tossing it to her. 'I suggest
you take a look at these before we go any further. That
way we can save both our time on lies.'

The envelope had fallen to the floor, spilling its con-
tents across the rug. Eden bent to pick up the photo-

graphs then felt her breath catch. Numbly, she gathered them together and stood up, flicking through them one by one, feeling shock rippling through her system.

Her eyes lifted to the man, their violet depths cloudy with confusion. 'Where . . . where did you get them?' she whispered.

He smiled tauntingly, his face filled with contempt. 'Where do you think, Miss Moore? Did you imagine that you would be safe in Edinburgh, free to enjoy your little liaison without fear that anyone would see you?' His mouth thinned, his eyes condemning. 'Out of sight of Rob's wife, who just happens to be my sister Becky?'

'But how . . .?'

'How did I find you?' He laughed harshly. 'I must admit it hasn't been easy. You and Rob covered your tracks extremely well these past weeks but Edinburgh was a mistake on more than one count. Not only did it prove that my suspicions were correct but you obligingly helped me identify you by signing the hotel register. Tracing you to this God-forsaken spot would have been almost impossible without that!'

Eden took a deep breath. She could hear the words she wanted to say inside her head, a logical, reasonable explanation which would clear up this whole misunderstanding at once. Yet as she looked at the photographs of the couple holding hands, kissing, the words wouldn't come.

How could she explain when she had no idea why Marcus Cole had come or what he wanted? How could she simply tell him the truth, that it wasn't her in these pictures but her sister, Eleanor, that it must have been Eleanor who had signed the hotel register in Eden's name when she'd known he intended to make trouble? She had loved and protected Eleanor since their parents had died and now more than ever she couldn't stop doing so when this grim-faced stranger had turned up with his as yet unvoiced threats!

The silence seemed to stretch, the wind dropping so that it seemed as if the world was waiting and holding its breath. Then, with a sudden surge, the storm regathered, pounding against the cottage walls. Drac whined in distress, butting his head against Eden's hip. She stroked him automatically, understanding his fears.

'What's the matter with him?'

She jumped at the sound of Cole's voice, glancing at him before looking hurriedly away, not liking the way he was watching her almost as though he could *see* inside her head. Until she knew what he wanted then she intended to keep her thoughts to herself!

'He was ill-treated, tied up during a storm and left.' She shrugged, running a soothing hand down the dog's back. 'He still gets nervous—but I doubt that you are really interested in hearing the full sorry tale. So, Mr Cole, shall we get down to the reason why you have come here?'

He raised a thick black brow. 'How astute of you to realise that we have things to discuss. I must say that you're a surprise in more ways than one.'

His gaze dropped to the photographs and a faint frown creased his brow as though something was puzzling him. Eden felt herself tense as she glanced down at the pictures. She and Eleanor were very alike despite the fact that she was two years older than her sister. They had the same colouring, the same delicate features, but how long would it take Cole to spot the differences now that he had chance to compare her with the woman in the pictures? That was something she couldn't allow to happen until she found out what he meant to do.

Shielding Eleanor from any unpleasantness had become second nature since she'd had that breakdown after their parents had died. Although Eleanor had recovered fully she had never been very stable since, the slightest pressure evoking rather wild behaviour. Recently she had been exhibiting signs of strain which had started Eden worrying about her health. A visit from Marcus Cole was the last thing Eleanor needed at present, when it could cause untold repercussions!

She slipped the photos back into their envelope and set them down on the dresser then gave the man a deliberately challenging stare. 'As I have even less idea of what you were expecting than the reason why you are here, I won't waste time worrying about it. So are you going to tell me what you want, Mr Cole?'

'I must say that you are handling this very well. Or is it simply that this isn't the first time you have found yourself in this situation? Although you don't fit my mental image of a *femme fatale*, I must confess.'

His eyes made a slow, insulting study of her slender figure in the bulky clothing then lingered on her make-up-free face. Eden wasn't vain. She had accepted years ago that she could never be classed as beautiful, unaware that her flawless milky white skin, deep violet eyes and thick glossy hair held an appeal which had caused more than one man to take a second look. Yet she deeply resented the way Marcus Cole was scrutinising her this way and evidently finding her lacking!

She glared at him, ignoring the way that sardonic brow lifted a fraction further. 'Just what do you want?'

'To ensure that you don't cause any more damage than you already have.'

'I haven't done a thing!'

'What do you call starting an affair with another woman's husband? Perhaps you class that as nothing, Miss Moore, but I don't!' He took a step towards her, bending so that he could stare straight into her eyes, sending an unwanted shiver of acknowledgement of his closeness rushing through her. 'My sister is crazy about Rob. It would break her heart if she ever found out about this, but I doubt you gave a second thought to how she would feel, did you? You set your sights on Rob and went after him with a single-minded determination, uncaring who got hurt in the process! I've got the whole story out of him so don't bother trying to lie. I didn't believe him at first when he told me that it had been *you* who'd pursued him, but I can see now that I should have given him the benefit of the doubt.'

'How dare you?' Eden's face was translucently pale, anger stealing every vestige of colour from her skin. There was no point in telling herself that the comments weren't really meant for her but Eleanor because it was she who was on the receiving end! She could feel Marcus Cole's contempt, hear the scorn coating each icy word so that they cut like a lash and awoke old memories which weren't buried deep enough to make her immune to the pain they aroused.

'Oh, I dare all right. I dare say that and a whole lot more. I don't give a damn about your *injured* feelings, Miss Moore, but I do care about my sister, and right at this moment I don't want anything upsetting her! Understand?'

Eden flinched from his anger. 'Look, Mr...'

'No, you look! Becky is pregnant.' He laughed harshly, watching Eden with cruel, unforgiving eyes. 'I don't expect it makes a scrap of difference to you to learn that. You went into this with your eyes wide open and I doubt that the thought of a child would have made you reconsider so long as you got what you wanted!'

'Tha—that is a dreadful thing to say!' she whispered hoarsely.

'Because it's true? You took what you wanted without a thought for the pain you would be causing but I won't allow you to ruin Becky's life with your selfishness.' His voice dropped an octave, running in vibrant discord along Eden's raw nerves so that she could feel it in every cell.

She drew back, feeling violated in some way, as though this man, this hard, arrogant stranger, had touched a deeply hidden core. 'So what do you propose, Mr Cole? I imagine you do have something in mind, some sort of punishment or penance?'

She laced her voice with sarcasm, refusing to let him see how shaken she was. What had Eleanor been thinking of to get into this dreadful mess? Oh, she'd known that her sister's relationship with her fiancé, Ben, had been going through a difficult patch a few months ago, but to get involved with another man, and a married one at that! If it came out then it could mean the end for Eleanor and Ben just when she'd hoped they were working things out.

Before Eleanor had met Ben she had been out with a lot of men, most of them highly unsuitable, but Ben was different. He really loved Eleanor and had managed to curb her rather headstrong ways with tenderness, and Eden had always believed that her sister loved him too. Had Eleanor really thought about what she was doing and the effect it would have? Probably not. She had a tendency to jump into things without thinking them through, might even now be bitterly regretting her impulsive behaviour. Ben would be deeply hurt but if

Eleanor told him herself about this affair with Lewis then maybe he would be able to forgive her because he loved her? But if Marcus Cole turned up at their house with his cold accusations there would be no chance of that happening! It was yet another reason why Eden knew she must make sure that Cole continued to think her the culprit, but it didn't make it any easier to stand there and bear the brunt of his contempt.

'Come along, Mr Cole. Don't be shy.' She laughed tauntingly, alarm racing through her when she saw the way his eyes narrowed, but she was determined to give Eleanor the chance to sort the mess out rather than have it sorted out for her! 'I doubt that shyness is something you're known for.'

He smiled suddenly, white teeth gleaming against tanned skin, grey eyes full of sardonic amusement. 'How quickly you seem to be getting to understand me. Good. It will save a lot of time, mine in having to convince you that I mean every word I say and yours in trying to accept it.'

She wasn't sure she liked the way the conversation was shifting but refused to let him see her unease. 'I'm all for saving time if it means we can bring this meeting to an end. So let's hear it, Mr Cole.'

'I want your word that you won't try to see or speak to Rob again.'

'I see. All right, Mr Cole, you have my word. Now, if that's all . . .' Eden turned to the door in relief but he made no attempt to leave.

'Not quite. I think it only fair that I should make it perfectly plain what will happen if you decide to break your promise.'

'Are you threatening me?' Eden strove to control the sudden panic that the cold statement evoked, standing stiff and erect as she faced him.

'Just offering a word or two of advice which will make your life far pleasanter.' He looked round again, taking his time in studying the simple furnishings which Eden had spent so much time and care on. The cottage had been a shell when she had found it and it had taken months of painstaking work to make it habitable again. But the hours of hard work had been the therapy she'd needed so desperately at the time.

'You see, I've done my homework on you, Miss Moore, and it's been quite a revelation. It's been— what?—almost two years since you hit the headlines? But the Press has a long memory so time is immaterial. Of course, you could be classed as simply unlucky that there was nothing more important happening in the world at that time, otherwise I doubt your story would have merited more than an inch of newsprint. But that's how it goes.' He smiled with false sympathy. 'You might enjoy the fame again but I doubt it, when you have apparently gone to so much trouble to hide yourself away here, even taken to using your maiden name again. I wonder if Rob knows your story? But that isn't really my business, I suppose. You keep your side of our bargain and no one will ever hear about it, but break your word and reporters will be beating a path to your door.'

'You bastard!' Eden was trembling, anger and humiliation coursing through her. There was no point in telling herself that it had all been lies, every word the tabloids had churned out, all that cruel, destructive speculation. It had hurt!

'I'm sure my mother would hotly dispute that but I can understand that you might be upset. The press coverage of your husband's death is something I'm sure you wouldn't want to be raked over again.'

'You know it isn't! That's why you mean to use it to... to blackmail me!' She laughed shrilly, hysteria edging closer to the surface. How bitterly ironic that by trying to protect Eleanor she'd put herself in jeopardy! 'But aren't you being just a bit too clever? Do you imagine your sister would relish having her name bandied about the papers if the story does come out?'

'"Blackmail" is far too dramatic a term. As for Becky's being involved in any unsavoury publicity, that won't happen. I have the contacts to make sure of that.' He shrugged lightly, obviously unconcerned by the thought. 'Still, hopefully it won't be necessary to go that far, Miss Moore. Stay away from Rob and you won't hear another word from me. But keep on with your sordid little affair and, believe me, you will regret it!'

He strode to the door and left without a backward glance. Eden ran and shot the bolt, leaning against the solid wood as her legs started to buckle. She'd tried so hard to put it all behind her, even told herself that she'd succeeded, but within the space of half an hour her life had been torn apart again!

She sank down on to the floor, looping an arm around the dog's neck when he came and nuzzled her. Hot, bitter tears were stinging her eyes but she couldn't cry. Marcus Cole's contempt and cruelty had scored too deeply for tears to provide a release.

CHAPTER TWO

EDEN had no idea how long she remained crouched by the door before slowly Drac's whining got through to her. She scrambled stiffly to her feet and stroked him. 'It's all right boy. Everything is going to be all right,' she murmured, yet the reassurance was meant as much for herself as for the dog.

She looked round the small room, her gaze lingering on the rough-cast walls she'd painted the palest shade of blue, the rag rugs which brightened the stone floor. She'd hung some of her paintings on the wall behind the table, seascapes which showed the Atlantic in every one of its varying moods. Usually just looking around the home she'd made soothed her, but the magic didn't work now. Marcus Cole had broken the spell, tainting the cottage, her refuge, with his presence.

Eden shut her eyes to try to rid herself of the feeling that he was still there but all that she succeeded in doing was conjuring up an image of him, his harshly handsome face filled with contempt, those cold grey eyes full of loathing. He hated her for what he believed she had done yet she'd been unable to explain her innocence, and that left behind a bitter taste she'd grown familiar with. She was no more guilty this time than last, and had just as little chance of proving it.

She walked over to the fire and started to bank it up for the night, her mind racing. She would have to get in touch with Eleanor as soon as possible and tell her what had happened then make her promise never to see Rob

Lewis again. If she could do that then this should be the
first and last time she would have to see Cole, which
would be some compensation. Perhaps he felt he had a
valid reason for what he had done but Eden would never
forgive him for the way he had gone about it!

It was Drac's insistent whining and clawing at the door
which eventually drew her attention. She glanced at him
and frowned. It was unusual for him to want to go out
again at this time but perhaps Cole's visit had upset him
as much as it had upset her.

Eden let him out but instead of doing what he had to
and coming back in out of the storm he ran to the bottom
of the path and started whining furiously.

'Drac come here!' she ordered impatiently, but he ignored her, running up the path a short way before racing
back and whining again. It was obvious that he wanted
her to follow him and she sighed as she unhooked her
yellow oilskin jacket off the back of the door. If he had
scented a rabbit and was getting her out there on some
wild-goose chase he was going to find himself very
unpopular!

The wind tore the hood off her head the minute she
stepped through the door. Eden caught the flying ends
of her hair and tucked them into the jacket collar,
bending into the wind as she followed the dog up the
steep path. It was dark outside, the light from the oil-
lamps in the cottage not strong enough to cut through
the inky gloom. Afterwards, Eden knew that if Drac
hadn't stopped and started pawing at something lying
on the ground then she would have carried right on past.

'Good dog. Good boy. Sit.'

She stopped dead, her heart hammering as she recognised the deep voice. For a moment she couldn't seem
to move, rooted to the spot by the shock of hearing

Marcus Cole's voice again, but then he swore roughly with undisguised impatience.

'In the name of heaven, woman, don't just stand there! Do something. You can start by helping me up!'

Eden took a quick little breath to control the rapidly rising panic and hurried towards the figure slumped on the ground. 'What—what happened? Are you all right?'

'Do I look all right? I'm hardly lying here admiring the view!' He bit off another oath as he tried to move, his eyes glittering with pain and anger. 'I fell when a section of this damned path gave way. I must have twisted my ankle.'

'Are you sure?' She pushed Drac away and bent down beside him. 'It might be broken.'

'No, I am not sure! I am not a doctor, Miss Moore. However, I do know that it hurts like hell and that I can't walk. So now that we've established the facts, few though they are, help me up!'

He held his arm out but Eden shot to her feet and backed away. He sank back, breathing heavily as he cursed slowly and methodically under his breath. Now that her eyes had grown accustomed to the dark she could see the tension in the set of his strong jaw, the thinness of his lips which spoke of pain. She should do something to help but she found it impossible to touch him after what had happened between them before.

'I can't stay out here all night,' he said in a reasonable tone. 'It might be almost summer but it's cold and wet and in an hour or so I'll be suffering from exposure. I need you to help me because I can't manage by myself.'

How had he known what she was feeling, this strange reluctance? Eden had no idea but it shook her to realise that Marcus Cole could understand her feelings. She took a hesitant step towards him then stopped again as more doubts surfaced. She'd made the cottage her sanctuary and already tonight this man had violated it. Could she really put at risk everything she'd achieved?

'Eden.' His voice was soft yet it sent vibrations skimming through her whole body. When he said her name in that way her heart beat a shade faster, her blood flowed a degree more warmly, her breathing deepened. It shocked her so much that she looked straight at him and found her eyes locking with his, held there by the glitter in those fathomless grey depths...

She rasped in a shuddery breath and bent to loop his arm across her shoulders, more afraid at that moment of all the odd sensations stirring to life inside her than of anything else. His hand, when she touched it, was icy, his body racked with shivers as it came into contact with hers, and all else faded in the face of practicality.

'See if you can stand when I take your weight,' she instructed briskly.

He made no attempt to answer, conserving his strength for the moment when he pushed himself off the ground. A faint gasp escaped his tightly drawn lips, but that was all, as he stood swaying perilously on one leg, keeping the injured foot clear of the ground. Eden studied him with concern, noting the sheen of perspiration on his brow, the tautness of his jaw, but before she could ask if he was all right he spoke abruptly.

'Well, what are we waiting for? Let's get this over with.'

Her mouth snapped shut as her temper rose a notch. Even now he was issuing his orders and expecting her to obey, but they would do this her way or not at all! She would get him back to the cottage, take a look at his ankle, maybe even offer him a cup of tea, if the milk of human kindness hadn't entirely dried up. Then she would get rid of him as fast as she could!

It had taken Eden just minutes to walk up the path but it took almost thirty to help Cole back down. Every step was an effort for both of them so that by the time they staggered through the door she was trembling with exertion. He was a big man, well-built and powerfully muscular, and despite the fact that he had done his utmost to help himself she'd had to support him bodily.

Helping him the last few feet to a chair, she eased him down then sagged beside him. He closed his eyes, his face grey beneath the tan, his breathing harsh and laboured. He'd not uttered a single word of complaint on the trek down the path despite the fact that she knew he must have been in a great deal of pain. He was tough to the core, a man who gave no concessions either to himself or others.

'I need to get out of these wet clothes. You'll have to help me.'

Colour swept up her cheeks when Eden suddenly realised that his eyes were open and he was watching her studying him! She muttered something which must have made some sense because he looked away and began to struggle his arms out of the sodden coat. Eden bent to help him, dragging it out of the way when he managed to raise himself off the seat.

She carried it across the room and hung it on the peg then turned back in time to see him shedding his suit jacket. He tossed it on to the floor then turned his attention to the shirt, tossing that on to the pile as well.

In the flickering light from the fire his skin gleamed like bronze, whorls of dark body hair covering his broad chest before arrowing down to his belt. Eden stopped abruptly, her heart performing the most crazy feats of acrobatics at the sight he made sitting there half dressed.

He must have noticed her reaction because he smiled with open mockery. 'Come, come, Miss Moore. This can't be the first time that a man has stripped off in front of you so I won't waste my breath on meaningless apologies. Perhaps you have something I could put on... a robe or something along those lines which you happen to have lying around?'

He made it sound as though she would have a store of such items, left there by any number of male guests! Eden glared at him then turned and ran swiftly up the narrow, enclosed staircase to her bedroom. She was sorely tempted to offer him a robe all right, one which usually languished at the back of her wardrobe. She had sold or given away most of her sophisticated wardrobe before moving to the cottage but some impulse had made her keep the violet silk with its trim of marabou around the neck. Now the thought of Marcus Cole decked out in it was enough to make her smile grimly!

Settling for a blanket instead, she went back downstairs and handed it to him without a word. He flung it around his shoulders and drew the ends across his chest, shuddering at its warmth. 'Thank you. I'd better take a look at this ankle and see how bad it is.'

He bent to remove his shoe, his face contorting on a spasm of pain as he tried to ease it off the swollen foot.

'Here, let me do it.' Eden knelt down on the floor and unlaced his shoe completely before carefully trying to ease it off, but even then she heard him gasp. She paused in concern, noting the pallor of his face.

'For God's sake get on with it!' he snapped.

He had to be the rudest, most insufferable man she'd ever met! Sitting there in *her* chair, in *her* house and giving *her* orders! Anger must have made her rougher than she'd meant to be because suddenly his hand clamped on her shoulder, long fingers biting through her thick woollen sweater.

'Take it easy, can't you? That isn't a lump of meat you're handling!'

Sweat was beaded across his forehead but Eden's sympathy had been sorely stretched and now snapped. 'I'm well aware of that! But just remember that this is your own fault, Mr Cole! If you hadn't come here tonight throwing your weight about, then you wouldn't be suffering the consequences!'

Contempt etched itself into every pain-filled line of his face. 'And if you had kept your hands off another woman's husband then there would have been no need for me to come.'

'But I didn't——' She stopped abruptly. The time to protest her innocence was long past. And what did it matter anyway what he thought of her? Yet she couldn't deny the pain she felt that he believed her capable of such a thing.

Without a word she set about the task of removing his shoe and sock but what she found made her heart sink even further. The ankle was badly bruised and swollen to double its size. It seemed unlikely that Marcus Cole would be able to walk on it for some time, and that left them exactly where? She could hardly throw him out in the middle of the storm but the alternative didn't bear thinking about!

Desperate to find a remedy, Eden got up and went into the kitchen to soak a towel in cold water then went back and wrapped it around his ankle. 'We'll see if that does any good in taking the swelling down.'

He smiled thinly. 'I doubt it's going to work miracles. I'm not going to be able to walk on it tonight.'

'We'll have to wait and see.' She looked away from those cold grey eyes, trying not to dwell on what he'd said. 'I'll make some tea while we wait.'

He stopped her when she went to walk away, his hand closing around the delicate bones in her wrist to jerk her to a halt. 'I don't like this any more than you do but there isn't much we can do about it.' He shrugged so that the blanket slipped from his shoulders, leaving the upper part of his body bare. The firelight played across his skin, highlighting the hard planes, the curve of muscle over bone, and something inside Eden reacted to the sight in a way which frightened her.

She tried to wrench herself free but instead of letting her go Marcus held her, his grip tightening as he watched her with narrowed eyes. 'Forget it! Whatever crazy ideas are running through your head, you can forget them.'

He let her go so suddenly that she had to steady herself against the edge of the table then clung on harder when he continued in the same cutting tone, 'I'm not that desperate for a woman that I would set my sights on you!'

Eden turned and hurried into the kitchen, closing the door on his tormenting laughter, wondering why she felt the sudden urge to cry. It shouldn't matter what Marcus Cole thought of her but it did. The ironic thing was that he had been so wrong just now in his suppositions. He thought she'd been afraid that he might make some sort of sexual advances to her, but that wasn't what had scared her at all. What had frightened her was her own, inexplicable reaction to the sight of him sitting there in the firelight, his powerful body half bare. She had thought herself immune to such feelings yet she'd looked at him just now and experienced, for the first time in years, a surge of raw desire. And that was something to be afraid of!

The next hour passed in an uncomfortable silence which neither of them made any attempt to break. Small talk was out of the question with the memory of why Cole had come lying between them. Eden glanced at the clock then set her cup aside and knelt down to unwrap the compress from his ankle but if anything the injury looked worse, the skin tight and shiny from the swelling, the darkness of a massive bruise discolouring the distended flesh.

'So, what is your opinion, Nurse?' he asked sarcastically. 'Think I'll be ready to run a four-minute mile in another hour or so?'

Eden got to her feet, barely looking at him as she took a deep breath and faced up to what had to be faced. 'You aren't going to be able to walk on that, let alone run. You'll have to spend the night here.'

He tilted his head back against the chair, watching her from beneath half-closed lids. 'That seems the only option. I apologise for inconveniencing you this way, Miss Moore. Given the choice I would never have set foot over your doorstep again.'

'And given the choice I would have you out of here this minute, so let's not waste our breath on meaningless platitudes!'

'A woman after my own heart who's not afraid to call a spade a spade. I really didn't think that we would have so much in common before I came here.'

Amusement echoed in the deep tones and she glared at him, violet eyes stormy with dislike. 'You and I have nothing in common, Mr Cole! And I shall give up a daily prayer of thanks for that! Now, do you think you'll

be able to make it upstairs by yourself or shall I need
to help you?'

'Oh, I wouldn't dream of putting you to so much
trouble.' His voice was smooth now yet it held a note
which made Eden stiffen in readiness for what was to
come. 'I couldn't possibly deprive you of your bed, and
I'm sure that I'm right to assume you weren't offering
to share it with me?'

'I most certainly wasn't!' she snapped back, hating
the fact that she could feel heat creeping up her neck at
the very thought.

He laughed derisively. 'Blushing, Miss Moore? How
delightfully old-fashioned. Yet I should have thought a
woman like you would be well past that.'

It was difficult to hide the hurt that his deliberate
cruelty evoked, but Eden did her best. 'I doubt you know
the first thing about a "woman like me". Oh, perhaps
you think you have all the answers but you could be
surprised to discover how wrong you are.'

'I doubt that.' He sounded suddenly bored, his gaze
moving past her. 'Anyhow, I shall be perfectly all right
here. If you would just move that stool closer then I can
rest my leg on it. That's all I need.'

Eden took a steadying breath which didn't quite
control the stabbing pain. She picked up the stool and
positioned it in front of the chair, watching while he
made himself comfortable then closed his eyes without
bothering to wish her goodnight.

She turned away, crossing the room to turn off the
oil-lamp on the dresser, then went to the one on the table,
lowering the flame until it cast just the faintest glow
across the room. The shadows deepened at once, as
though someone had taken a paintbrush and swiftly filled
in the corners of a canvas so that only the central figure

stood out...Marcus Cole sitting in her chair in the middle of her living-room...suddenly thrust into the middle of her life!

Dawn came in as a surge of red and gold running across the black sky. Eden lay in bed watching the shadows fleeing before the light. She'd barely slept and when she had her dreams had been haunted with old memories and new mixed into one kaleidoscope of images which had left her tossing restlessly. Now she got up and thrust open the window, drinking in the tangy, salt-laden air.

The storm had tossed fresh debris on to the small, stony beach at the bottom of the cliff, chunks of driftwood bleached and gnarled from immersion in the sea water. It would be a good day to go scavenging for any suitable pieces she could use in her sculptures but that depended on how soon she could get rid of her un-wanted guest.

Her mouth thinned at the thought of the man down-stairs and she closed the window with a sharp thud then collected clean clothes and hurried into the tiny bathroom to shower. There were just two rooms upstairs in the cottage—her bedroom and the bathroom. Before Eden had bought the place there had been no indoor plumbing despite the previous occupants—a fisherman and his wife plus their five children—having lived there for years!

Dressed at last in her usual jeans and a thick oyster wool sweater, she ran downstairs, making no attempt to muffle her footsteps. If Marcus Cole was still asleep then hard luck. The sooner he was awake and on his way the better. However, there was no sign of him when she reached the bottom step.

Puzzled, Eden looked round but there were no hiding places in the small room. Had he left already without bothering to tell her he was going? Perhaps she should feel annoyed at such a lack of courtesy but frankly it seemed like a blessing!

Humming softly to herself in relief at being spared another confrontation, Eden walked into the kitchen—and stopped dead. In a shocked sweep her gaze ran the length of the man's bare back, rushed over tautly muscular flanks beneath dark boxer shorts, flew on down yards of powerful leg then jumped back to his face just as Marcus Cole turned awkwardly around.

'I hope you don't mind me using the kitchen sink to get cleaned up?'

Eden swallowed down the rest of the tune, feeling every crotchet inching its way back down her dry throat so that it seemed to take eons before she could force any words out. 'I... No, of course not,' she muttered thickly.

Cole nodded curtly, letting the water run out of the sink before looking around for a towel to dry himself with. He reached for the one hooked behind the door then cursed softly as he inadvertently stepped on to his injured foot. 'Can you pass me that towel, please?'

His tone turned the request into an order but for once Eden was only too pleased to obey. Hurriedly she unhooked the towel, using the few seconds it took to get herself under control. It was ridiculous to act as though she'd never seen a near-naked man before! After all, she had been married for two years and before that had drawn the naked male body on numerous occasions in art classes. She knew how each muscle worked, was familiar with the shapes and textures which made up the wonder of the human body. Yet when she turned around to hand Cole the towel she knew that she had rarely seen such perfection!

He ran the towel over his wet black hair then draped it around his neck while he finger-combed the damp strands back from his forehead. There were droplets of water caught in the hair which feathered across his chest, the sheen of dampness on his shoulders and down his arms. It highlighted the curve of muscle honed to perfection and Eden felt again that crazy, alarming, *maddening* feeling that she'd felt the night before!

She gave some sort of muttered excuse and turned to leave, but he stopped her. 'You don't need to go. I shall be through here in a moment or two. Just carry on with whatever you wanted to do.' He laughed suddenly in a way which made the heat rush through her veins. 'I'm not at all shy about letting you see me like this, Eden. And I'm quite sure it doesn't bother you one bit . . . does it?'

And what could she say to that? Yes and no were the two simplest words in the English language yet deciding which one to choose right now was like tiptoeing through a minefield.

In the end Eden said nothing, merely shooting Cole a speaking look as she stepped around him and filled the kettle, praying that he wouldn't notice just how her hands were shaking. But she should have realised there was little he ever missed!

'Are you always this jumpy around people, or do I merit special treatment?'

There went another yes and no question she had no intention of touching! She lifted crockery out of the cupboard and headed for the door, only to find him somehow in her way. 'Excuse me. I want to lay the table.' She stared pointedly at the door but he made no attempt to move aside.

He smiled assessingly, grey eyes taking lazy stock of her face. 'When you've answered my question, Eden.'

'I am sure you can answer it yourself, *Mr* Cole! And I don't think it will take too much thinking about either.'

'I'm sure I can, at least partially. Naturally you aren't too kindly disposed towards me, seeing as I intend to end your dalliance with Rob. Yet I have the oddest feeling that isn't the only reason why you're so jittery around me.' He reached out the mere inch or so it took to tilt her chin and held it so that she was forced to bear his scrutiny. 'It intrigues me, Eden, makes me ask myself why you are so on edge, and if it's because you're trying to keep something from me.'

He was far too perceptive and somehow she had to deflect his interest rather than run the risk of him hitting upon the truth! 'Such as? You seem to know everything there is to know about me, don't you, Mr Cole? As for being intrigued... well, I should have thought there was little you would find intriguing about my lifestyle when it's an open book to you.'

His eyes narrowed, glittering grey slits of ice. 'I have always made it a rule to find out about an opponent, all his... or her... weaknesses and vulnerabilities.' He shrugged lightly but his gaze was just as intent, just as searching. 'I thought I had found out everything about you from all those newspaper articles but none of them told me what goes on inside that beautiful head of yours, and that's what fascinates me.'

'Beautiful?' She gave a harsh little laugh, feeling afraid. She didn't want to incite any more of his curiosity. She just wanted him out of her life before he destroyed everything she'd worked so hard to achieve! 'Don't tell me you're going to resort to flattery now? You do disappoint me. Threats are more your style, Mr

Cole, so stick to them and leave the compliments to those who really mean them!'

She pushed past him, uncaring that she almost knocked him off balance. She hurried into the living-room and started to lay the table, her hands shaking as she arranged the crockery. How she hated him! Hated him for his insufferable attitude, his prying and probing, the threat he represented to her. She'd thought that those dreadful days when her life had been almost destroyed by lies were over, yet Marcus Cole was rapidly opening old wounds and adding fresh ones!

The temptation to tell him the truth just to get rid of him was suddenly so great that Eden actually started back to the kitchen before slowly the implications of such an action seeped through her anger. How could she tell him when it was tantamount to giving him a licence to ruin Eleanor's life? It wouldn't even change Cole's opinion of her, because that was based as much on what he had read in the newspapers as anything else, but it would surely mean the end of Eleanor's relationship with Ben if Marcus Cole turned up with his accusations! Eleanor had been wrong to get into this affair, but if there was a chance that something could be salvaged from the mess, then Eden meant to give it to her.

When Marcus Cole came into the room and awk-wardly made his way to where his clothes were, Eden turned back to laying the table without uttering a word and remained silent until breakfast was on the table.

'Breakfast is ready.'

'You needn't have bothered going to any trouble on my account,' he said coolly, hobbling slowly to the table to sit down.

He made it sound as though she'd deliberately tried to wheedle her way into his good books, and that annoyed her! 'I didn't. I was making breakfast for myself anyway.' She pulled out a chair then glanced round as she suddenly missed Drac.

With that alarming perception he exhibited, Marcus understood at once. 'He wanted to go out so I let him. I hope that was all right?'

'Of course. He never goes far.'

As though on cue there was a scratching at the door. Eden went to open it, staggering back as the huge dog leapt joyfully up at her. He was always absurdly glad to see her, as though half afraid that she might disappear like his previous owner who had left him tied up and starving when he'd moved house.

Eden fussed him then went to fill his dish, glancing round when he didn't follow her, stunned to see him rushing round the table to Marcus. Drac had an in-built distrust of strangers, and of men in particular, yet he seemed to have forged a bond with Marcus Cole. Perhaps that old belief that animals were good judges of character wasn't true after all!

Breakfast was eaten in total silence, which was only broken when Eden got up to load the dirty dishes on to the tray. Marcus handed her his cup then leant back in the chair, watching her as though he found something puzzling about the domestic scene. 'Has Rob ever stayed here with you?'

The tray lurched, clattering the dishes together. Eden steadied it carefully, suddenly wary of where this was leading. 'No.'

'I thought not.' At her enquiring glance, he elaborated with a cynical smile, 'Rob has a great fondness for luxury and I can't imagine this being his sort of setting at all. So, where do you and he meet—at a hotel here in Cornwall, or do you travel up to London for your little trysts?'

Eden bit back a groan, wondering how long she could play this role without giving herself away. She had no idea at all about clandestine meetings! 'I...I travel up to London once or twice a month,' she improvised, although it was a perfectly truthful answer in many respects.

'And where do you stay? Different hotels each time?' he probed relentlessly. 'Or do you have your own "special" place where you know you won't be disturbed?'

How she hated that cruel mockery in his voice which somehow managed to make her *feel* guilty even though she wasn't! 'I don't think that's any of your business. What do you want, Mr Cole, a blow-by-blow account of what goes on behind the bedroom door? Is that the way you get your thrills?' Her voice was laced with scorn and she saw his eyes glitter with anger yet suddenly she was recklessly unconcerned. 'Perhaps you did too much research on me...all those articles in the tabloids must have wetted your appetite. Would you like to know if I'm as good in bed as I'm reputed to be?'

He stood up, towering over her because they were so close. 'I have no appetite whatsoever for you, Eden Moore. Just the thought of the kind of woman you are sickens me, if you'd like the truth.' His eyes skimmed her from head to toe, contempt acidly etched in their grey depths. 'The thing which makes me curious, though, is that I cannot imagine that you suit Rob's taste either. It makes me think that I'm missing something. I wonder what it is?'

She forced herself to meet his disdainful gaze, telling herself it didn't matter what he thought of her so long as he didn't arrive at the truth. If he discovered the mistake he'd made then it would be so much worse for Eleanor because his anger would know no bounds. Marcus Cole wasn't the kind of man who would take kindly to being misled! Yet sticks and stones couldn't have inflicted as much pain as those harsh, condemning words.

'What could you possibly have missed? I imagine you have the complete picture, Mr Cole, so I cannot see there is anything to add.'

She picked up the tray and started towards the kitchen, slowing when behind her Marcus said softly, 'Oh, I thought I had. I was fairly confident that I knew the score but now I'm not quite so certain. There are things which don't add up about this whole situation, Eden. Still, no matter. I'm sure I shall get to the bottom of it. One thing I never could resist was unravelling a mystery.'

Eden carried on into the kitchen without saying a word and ran water into the bowl as she stared out across the sea and watched the tide drawing away from the shore. If only she could run down to the beach and let the tide carry her away, far, far away from Marcus Cole and all the threats he represented to her!

CHAPTER THREE

THERE was absolute silence in the room. Eden bit her lip as she watched Marcus Cole take a few tentative steps before sitting down abruptly on a chair. She'd torn up an old sheet and bound his ankle tightly but that painfully short attempt proved conclusively that he wasn't going anywhere just yet. So where did that leave them? She hesitated to make a guess!

He looked up at her, his face grey with strain yet his mouth curled into that cynical smile she was growing to know so well. 'I can almost hear your brain ticking over, Eden, wondering how much longer you'll have to put up with me.' He laughed when she looked away. 'No, don't feel guilty! I have no more desire to outstay my welcome than you have to prolong it. However, there is a solution if you're prepared to give it a go. Can you drive?'

'I . . . yes,' she replied hesitantly. 'Of course I can.'

'Then the answer to both our problems is for you to drive me back to town.' He ran a hand impatiently through his black hair. 'God knows I can't spend any more time down here! I've a case coming to court next week which needs all the attention I can give it and I've already wasted far too much time recently on one thing and another!'

Why did she have the sudden unshakable feeling that she was the 'other'? Eden glared at him. 'Don't try blaming me! I didn't ask you to start poking your nose into my life.'

'Not in so many words, but you set the wheels in motion three months ago when you took up with Rob.'

Had it really been going on so long? She could scarcely believe it, yet when she thought about it Eleanor had been keyed up for some time now. She had simply put it down to the rough patch Eleanor was going through with Ben, and the fact that her sister never handled any emotional pressure well, but it appeared there was another explanation.

Suddenly Eden became aware that Marcus was speaking. She cast him a quick look, seeing the way his mouth compressed into a thin line of annoyance.

'No point in asking where your thoughts were wandering, but just make sure that's all that happens.' He gave a harsh laugh which made her flinch. 'I can't stop you thinking about Rob, I suppose, but I can and will do everything in my power to stop you seeing him again! Make no mistake of that.'

The sudden surge of anger she felt was a blessing as it helped conceal the pain she felt at his deliberate taunts. 'I'm not stupid, Mr Cole. I'm fully aware that it would give you a great deal of satisfaction, if not pleasure, to be able to carry out your nasty threats.'

She swung round and walked stiffly to the stairs, barely pausing when behind her Marcus called her name. She glanced back at him, chilled to the bone by the icy contempt which lay over his face like a mask.

'It would indeed. How well you know me. But I keep my word, Eden. Play fair with me and I shall play fair with you, probably fairer than you deserve.' He shot a glance at his watch and frowned. 'I need to be back in London this afternoon, so when can we get going?'

'Just as soon as I've changed.' She laughed hollowly. 'Believe me, you can't be any more eager to leave than I am to get rid of you!'

She ran up the stairs, almost childishly pleased to have got the last word for once, something she had a feeling rarely happened around Cole. As quickly as she could she changed into 'city' clothes—a smart black suit with a lavender blouse. She brushed her hair then caught it back with a hand-painted silk scarf in shades of lavender and rose, slipping silver hoop earrings into her lobes. Medium-height leather shoes and bag completed the outfit and she was back downstairs in less than fifteen minutes.

Marcus was standing by the window when she stepped from the bottom stair. He turned slowly, taking his weight on his good ankle while he subjected her to an uncomfortably thorough scrutiny. He smiled slowly in a way which made Eden shift nervously before she stopped herself.

'So at last I get to see the real woman. Now I think I can see just what attracted Rob to you and why he found it so difficult to refuse your attentions.'

He turned the compliment into a cool insult, his voice grating with derision. Eden drew herself up, glad of the high heels which brought her almost on eye level with him. 'Then at least you've solved that mystery which was bothering you. Now if you are ready and have finished paying me your own particular brand of *compliment*, shall we go?'

She took his arm, feeling the immediate tensing of his muscles beneath her fingers, evidence of how much he disliked her touching him. Eden blanked that oddly painful thought, matching her pace to his as she helped him up the steep path to the sleek black BMW parked on the grass at the top.

He braced himself against the wall and felt in his pocket for the keys, tossing them to her. Eden unlocked the doors then helped him inside before slipping behind the wheel. She ran a glance over the dashboard to acquaint herself with the layout then turned to Cole to ask if there was anything she needed to know about driving the powerful machine. However, he had his head back against the seat, his eyes closed, his face set and uncompromising. If he'd handed her written instructions he couldn't have made it clearer, but as far as she was concerned it suited her fine. She didn't want to indulge in meaningless conversation when they had nothing at all to say to one another!

It was noon when they drew up in front of the expensive block of flats where Marcus lived. Eden cut the engine then stretched wearily. It had been a long and tedious journey, made even more so by the atmosphere in the car. Now she couldn't wait to be on her way.

She shot Marcus Cole a quick look, colouring when she found him watching her. She looked away at once, watching another vehicle pull into the driveway and park a few yards away, then started nervously when he spoke for the first time since they'd set off.

'You were wrong, you know.'

'About what?' She eyed him warily, seeing the small half-smile which played at the corners of his masculinely beautiful lips and softened the harshness of his face for a second.

'About the mystery being solved. Oh, you do look the part now, granted: elegant, graceful, beautiful enough to make any man desire you. But you don't *act* like the *femme fatale* I was expecting.'

Eden laughed shortly. 'Because I haven't tried to charm you?' She gave a small shrug. 'Perhaps the simple answer is that I don't find you attractive, Marcus. I'm sorry if that is something of a blow to your ego.'

He laughed out loud, totally unperturbed. 'Perhaps that's it. But it still doesn't feel quite right somehow. According to Rob you are nothing short of a rampant man-eater, which is virtually the picture the papers painted of you. Yet even allowing for the fact that both were lying to some degree, Rob to try and excuse his behaviour and the tabloids to promote a sensational story, it still doesn't add up. I keep trying to match what I've read and been told with what I see and it's almost as though there are two people involved.'

Eden's heart rolled over. He was far too astute, that razor-sharp mind honing in on points that others would have missed. She had to allay his suspicions somehow to protect Eleanor. All her sister needed was a little time to sort herself out and she intended to give her that!

She let her mouth form a deliberately seductive smile, her voice soft and husky. 'Do you think it could be because you don't *want* to see me in that light, Marcus?'

His face hardened, grey eyes glacial as they swept over her with disdain. 'I don't think so. I imagine the simple answer is that you are a consummate actress, Eden Moore, a modern-day Cleopatra who can be "all things to all men". But I'm afraid it won't work with me because you leave me cold.'

'Do I?' She pouted at him, her heart aching as she saw the disgust in his eyes. Yet it was the one guaranteed way she knew to stop that dangerous train of thought. 'I'm sure I could change your mind, Marcus. After all, if I'm to be deprived of Rob's attentions then I will be in need of a little male...companionship.'

He didn't bother to reply, pushing the car door open and getting out awkwardly before Eden could help him. She took a shaky little breath, hating the way she'd been forced to act so out of character. Climbing out of the car, she forced herself to speak. 'Do you want me to help you inside?'

He shrugged aside her proffered hand, slipping the car keys into his pocket before drawing out his wallet. 'I can manage. I assume you will be travelling back by train?' At her nod he peeled several notes off the wad of money and offered them to her. 'This should cover your train fare and any out-of-pocket expenses.'

Eden put her hands behind her back in a gesture of refusal. 'No. I don't want your money.'

'Why should you lose out any more than you have to? After all, it's going to be enough of a blow having to do without those expensive treats I'm sure Rob gave you, although I imagine you'll soon find someone willing and eager to replace him.'

He made her sound like a gold-digger but it wasn't the first time that she'd been portrayed wrongly that way. Eden's temper rose on the back of a bitter resentment which even time hadn't managed to quite allay. Geoff, her husband, had been rich, his family part of the aristocracy. The papers had made much of the fact that she had come from a fairly modest background by comparison. The implication had been that she had married Geoff for his money, the twenty-year age-gap between them merely fuelling the speculation. It had been lies, of course, like all the rest that had been printed. She had married Geoff for many reasons, not least of which being because she'd thought she loved him. It was only later that she'd realised what a mistake she had made.

'Damn you, Marcus Cole! Who gave you the right to sit there on your pedestal and pass judgement? What makes you so sure...?'

'Marcus! Where have you been? I've been trying to get hold of you for days!'

Eden stopped at once, turning to see a small, dark-haired woman hurrying towards them. She linked her hand through Marcus's arm with a smile which didn't quite dispel the lines of tension on her pretty face. 'Honestly, you're harder to find than the invisible man lately!'

Marcus bent to kiss her cheek, a warning light in his eyes when he glanced at Eden which she couldn't understand. She had no idea who the woman was, nor much interest in finding out, yet somehow she knew that seeing her right now was the last thing that Marcus wanted.

'I've been away for a few days.'

'Tell me something I don't know!' The woman laughed. 'But where? And what have you been up to to get into that state?' She shot a mischievous look at his ruined suit then held her hand out to Eden. 'I think I'd better introduce myself, seeing as Marcus isn't about to. I'm Becky.'

'Becky?' Eden glanced at Marcus for confirmation and felt her heart sink at the expression on his face.

'My sister, Becky Lewis.' His voice was smooth as silk yet it sent a cold shudder vibrating down Eden's spine. Her eyes flew to the stoney grey depths of his, wondering what would happen next. It was one thing for Marcus to accuse her of having an affair with his sister's husband and quite another for it to come out in front of the woman! But he merely carried on smoothly with the introductions. 'Becky, I would like you to meet a friend of mine, Eden Moore.'

'Eden? You mean that *you* and Eden ... you two are ... are ...?' Becky's face was ashen, her eyes, a softer, warmer shade of grey than her brother's reflecting her shock. Eden had the feeling that she would have fallen if she hadn't been holding on to Marcus's arm.

She took an instinctive step towards Becky then stopped when the woman carried on in a rush which made little sense at first. 'Oh, I owe you such a huge apology, Eden! It was all a mistake, a silly misunderstanding, but now ...' Becky drew a small breath then smiled tremulously, glancing from Eden to her brother. 'I found this note, you see, one Eden must have written to you, and thought that it ... it belonged to Rob! I've been going through hell imagining that ... Well, it doesn't matter now, does it?' She reached out and clasped Eden's hand. 'I'm just so delighted for you and Marcus!'

Eden stood in stunned silence. She could feel the sun warm on her back yet she felt icily cold as she looked from Becky's smiling face to Marcus's set one and willed him to say something to set his sister right. She and Marcus weren't having any sort of relationship, let alone the sort Becky obviously imagined!

But the seconds ticked past, ran into minutes while the silence lengthened ...

'Why didn't you say *something*?'

'What precisely? I have no idea what was in that note even if you have, so how could I deny it?' Marcus sounded so cool and unmoved that Eden could happily have hit him if she hadn't had the feeling that he would retaliate without the slightest qualm.

She glared at him as she unplugged the coffee-maker and filled the china pot, setting it on the tray with the cups and saucers while the sheer incongruity of the situation hit her. Here she was in Marcus Cole's flat making coffee as though he and she really were the couple his sister believed them to be!

Her hands shook as she carried the tray into the large sitting-room and covertly glanced around for somewhere to put it without betraying that she didn't know her way around the place.

'Put it down by Becky, darling. She'll pour.'

Marcus's soft tone wasn't loud enough to startle her but the endearment was! Eden just managed to steady the listing tray before it fell, striving for an outward show of calm as she carried it across the room and set it down on the black ash table beside Becky's chair.

'Come and sit by me, sweetheart.'

Marcus patted the cushion next to him on the leather sofa, his mouth curved into a smile which didn't reach his eyes. Eden took a deep breath then went and sat down beside him, flinching as he slid an arm around her shoulders and drew her to him in an affectionate gesture which made her blood race—though purely from annoyance, she quickly told herself.

'So, Becky, do I take it that you've been trying to get hold of me because something has happened?'

Becky handed Eden a cup of coffee, presenting her with the perfect opportunity to free herself from Marcus as she leant forward to accept it. She sipped the coffee, watching as Becky poured another cup for herself with an unsteady hand. It was obvious that Becky still hadn't fully recovered from the shock she'd had and Eden felt a momentary stirring of compassion for her before ruthlessly telling herself that it was none of her business.

What she had to concentrate on now was extricating herself from this mess.

Becky took a deep breath and smiled shakily. 'Yes, but there's no need to worry that it's anything unpleasant. But tell me what has been happening to you first. How did you injure your ankle?'

Marcus shrugged dismissively. He'd excused himself while Eden was making the coffee, reappearing a short time later dressed in black trousers and a black cashmere sweater over a pale blue shirt. With his hair neatly brushed and his skin freshly shaven he looked once more the elegant, aloof stranger who had suddenly appeared out of the night. It was hard to believe that only hours before she had never even known of his existence; now Eden felt herself growing tense as she waited to hear what he would say.

'Sheer carelessness. I wasn't looking where I was going and slipped.' He glanced at Eden, his voice dropping so that it suddenly seemed to be deep and vibrant with meaning. 'I had other things on my mind at the time.'

Eden choked on a mouthful of coffee. She put the cup down, looking anywhere but at the man at her side, afraid that she would do something reckless. How dared he imply that he'd been thinking about her...and in that way? Any thoughts Marcus Cole might have had about her last night had been of a far different nature!

Becky laughed with delight, more of the strain easing from her face. 'You don't need to say anything more! I'm pretty sure I can fill in the rest myself, although I do wish you had told me about Eden before instead of being so secretive. It would have saved me from——' She stopped abruptly, looking faintly embarrassed. 'I'd better tell you the reason why I've been trying to find you, hadn't I?'

'If it's pleasant news then most definitely. I could do with some of that.' Marcus must have seen his sister's frown because he added smoothly, 'Injuring my ankle is going to be extremely inconvenient.'

'Of course, but hopefully Eden will be able to stay and look after you?'

Oh, this was getting worse by the second, one lie building on top of another until there was a mountain of them which threatened to cause an avalanche if either she or Marcus tripped up! Eden smiled non-committally and picked up her coffee to drink it and so avoid making any reply.

'I'm sure we shall be able to work something out,' Marcus said coolly. 'But come on, Becky, don't leave us in suspense. What is this news?'

'Natalie is getting married.' Becky laughed. 'Surprised? I was. But it's wonderful news. And I believe you know the man she is marrying, Marcus. His name is Flynn O'Rourke.'

'Yes, I know him.' Marcus's tone was flat and unrevealing yet Eden sensed a certain emotion under the level tones she couldn't quite pin down. She glanced at him, trying to work out what he was thinking, but that was impossible. A whole psychology textbook could be devoted to a man like him and still no one would understand his feelings unless he chose to let them!

'Then you must know how charming he is! I met him for the first time the other day; in fact, he and Natalie stayed the weekend with us, and I must say that I can understand why she fell for him. And it's obvious that he's crazy about her!'

'I see. Well, obviously that is wonderful news. And if anyone can take care of Natalie then O'Rourke can. So when is the wedding to take place?'

Had she been imagining things? Sensing emotions which didn't exist? Eden shot another glance at Marcus but couldn't decide and finally gave up the unequal struggle. After all, this forthcoming marriage was of little relevance to her and all the burgeoning problems in her life!

'Two weeks' time at the village church. I've told Natalie that I want to hold the reception at the house.' Becky glanced at Eden with a smile. 'Natalie and I have been best friends for years. She has no family now that the elderly aunt who brought her up is dead so it seemed fitting that she should get married at the place where she used to spend so much time when we were younger.'

'I'm sure she will appreciate that,' Eden replied. 'It's kind of you to go to so much trouble.'

'Oh, I'm looking forward to it, now more than ever, in fact!'

There was a note in Becky's voice which made it plain what she really meant. Whatever had been in that letter must have caused her a great deal of heartache. What a mess it all was: Eleanor and Rob; Marcus believing that *she*, Eden, was responsible; and now Becky's assumption that she and Marcus were involved!

Troubled, Eden glanced at Marcus, and saw by his expression that he was thinking much the same. His eyes were cold and condemning, chilling in their dislike as they focused on her. How he hated her for what he thought she'd done, and how powerless she was to tell him the truth!

'Natalie and Flynn don't want a big wedding. Just a few friends on both sides with Marcus and me almost as family. And I know she will be absolutely delighted that you'll be there, Eden.'

It was hard to hide her shock. 'Me? Oh, but I couldn't! It's awfully kind of you, but I really couldn't go...'

'Darling, there's no need to be shy, especially not in front of Becky.' Marcus's voice was warmly amused. He reached out and caught Eden's cold hand to lift it to his lips while he pressed a kiss to her knuckles, holding it while he smiled wryly at his sister.

'Eden and I have been trying to keep our relationship a secret for one reason and another which I won't go into right now. But, as you say, there will only be a handful of close friends at this wedding so there really isn't any reason why we should miss it.'

He rubbed her hand against his cheek in an intimate little caress which spoke volumes but said all the *wrong* things! Eden stared at him in horror, trying not to believe what she was hearing. Marcus couldn't possibly expect her to go to his sister's house and carry on with this charade!

'You will enjoy meeting everyone, darling. Natalie and Flynn—oh, and Rob, of course, Becky's husband.' Marcus laughed softly. 'I must have mentioned him to you, surely?'

Was she the only one to hear that nuance in his voice? Eden glanced at Becky but there was no trace of suspicion on the other woman's face. How could he do this? How could he use her as a pawn in this game of make-believe?

'I just don't think it would be right, *darling*. You forget that I've never met Natalie. She couldn't possibly want a stranger at her wedding!' She injected just a touch of scepticism into her voice as she fought against the panic clawing her insides. But it wasn't Marcus who answered this time.

'Nonsense! Natalie will be as thrilled about this wonderful news of you and Marcus as I was.' Becky stood up, beaming at them both, no signs of strain now on her face. 'Tonight is going to be a double celebration, in fact.' She laughed tenderly. 'And Rob could just be in for a shock when he finds out that he's going to become a father!'

'You haven't told him about the baby yet, then?' Marcus asked quietly, his eyes watchful.

Becky shook her head, faint colour stealing into her face. 'No. I...I thought it better to wait...until I was absolutely certain. Rob would have been so disappointed, you see.'

She turned to pick up her bag but not fast enough to conceal the flash of guilt in her eyes. Eden felt her heart ache for her. Obviously Becky had concealed the news of her pregnancy because she'd been unsure if she and Rob still had a future together. It left the onus lying even more on her: there wasn't only Eleanor's future to consider but Becky's and the baby's too. Yet by continuing with this masquerade she would blacken herself even more in Marcus's eyes and that was a bitterly painful thought.

'I must go now. I don't want to miss my train.' Becky bent to kiss Marcus then pushed him back into the seat when he made to get up. 'No, stay there and rest your ankle. Eden can see me out.'

With an expectant glance at Eden she headed for the hall, leaving her no choice but to follow. Yet before she opened the front door Becky stopped and pulled a folded sheet of paper from her bag.

'This belongs to you—or, rather, I suppose it belongs to Marcus. I must apologise for reading it, Eden. It wasn't intentional prying, just a simple misunderstanding. I found it on the floor under the living-room sofa and naturally assumed that Rob had dropped it, but of course it's obvious now that Marcus must have done so when he popped in to see me the other week.'

She handed it over with a mischievous grin. 'I must admit it was quite a revelation that my cool, calm, and oh, so together brother could inspire that amount of passion!'

Eden closed the door after Becky left and stared down at the paper with distaste. She had no desire to read it. She would prefer not to know what her sister had written. However, before she could rip it up as she intended a large hand reached over her shoulder and took it from her.

'Don't!' She spun round to glare at Marcus who was propped against the wall unfolding the note. 'That wasn't meant for you. You have no right to read it!'

'Seeing as I'm having to play the part of the recipient, I would dispute that. I prefer to see just what is expected of me.' He skimmed through the note then raised mocking eyes to her angry face. 'Well, well, who would have expected such an outpouring of emotion from you, my sweet little temptress? Is it any wonder poor old Rob found it difficult to resist what you so graphically offered? Makes me wonder what I've been missing all my life.'

How she hated him for that cold amusement, that icy mockery of other people's feelings! She reached out and snatched the note from him and thrust it into her pocket then stormed into the sitting-room to collect her things.

'Surely you aren't embarrassed, Eden? Such a fulsome outpouring of passion shows a certain talent. Or could it simply be that you had the chance to hone your skills on other alliances even before your husband died?'

She whirled to face him, eyes blazing in a face which was stark and white. 'Damn you! Who do you think you are to say that? Do you really imagine that you know anything at all about the life I led when I was married? All you've had to go on are those lurid newspaper articles, and what's written in the papers must be gospel! You can't see further than the print, can't see it for what it was—lies and more lies, fed to the Press by people who knew nothing!' She flung the strap of her bag over her shoulder. 'Your mind is just as warped as hi——'

She stopped abruptly, suddenly aware of what she was saying. Apart from Eleanor, no one knew the truth about her marriage, yet she'd come within a hair's breadth of telling Marcus Cole!

She headed for the door, so shaken that she couldn't even look at him. But he stopped her with a hard hand on her arm.

'If that was a bid for sympathy, Eden, then save your breath. I don't give a damn about your marriage or anything else you've done in the past! My only concern is Becky's future. She and Rob might just have a chance to make a go of things with you out of the way.' He laughed harshly, the taunting note grating on her raw nerves so that she felt sick. 'And what better way to convince him that your affair is over than to attend this wedding? Seeing you there with me should be all the proof he needs of that, not to mention the fact that it will help reinforce Becky's belief that you and I are a hot item! Frankly, this couldn't have worked out better if I had planned it.'

Eden twisted free, staring at him with huge, disbelieving eyes. 'You can't be serious. You don't honestly imagine that I will go?'

'Of course you will. You can't avoid it now that Becky is expecting you.'

'No! I won't do it! And you cannot make me, Marcus!'

His eyes turned almost black with the force of his anger as he bent towards her. 'Oh, but I can, and I will! I think you already know the consequences of crossing me. A word or two in the right ears and you'll be making headlines again.'

'You're despicable! I don't know how you can live with yourself if this is how you go about getting what you want from life!' She was trembling with tension, unable to believe that he would do this.

'I can live with myself just as easily as you can live with yourself. Perhaps we're more alike than I realised. We both go after what we want with a single-minded purpose.'

'Don't insult me! We are not at all alike. You are nothing but a ruthless bully and . . .'

'And you are Snow White, pure and guiltless? Sorry, sweetheart, but that is too much to swallow.' He studied her angry face. 'There's no point in discussing this further. You will attend Natalie's wedding and act the part you seem to have been cast in, even though I'm not overjoyed by the prospect either.'

'Part?' she queried numbly.

He cupped her cheek, his long fingers cool and firm on her heated flesh, his mouth curled into a derisive smile. 'The part you wrote for yourself with that note, Eden: my lover.'

There was a moment when her heart seemed to stop, when blood no longer flowed along her veins, when her breathing suspended, while she stared into his face until every line was imprinted on her memory. Then, with a sharp surge, her heart started to beat furiously, the blood flooded through her body and she tore herself away and ran from the flat. But she couldn't run from that one tormenting word which echoed relentlessly in her head on the long journey home. 'Lovers'... She and Marcus Cole... Never!

CHAPTER FOUR

THE sun was dipping towards the horizon by the time Eden stepped from the taxi. She paid the driver then made her way down the path, fussing over Drac when he bounded out to greet her as she unlocked the door.

Tossing her bag on to the table, she looked around her haven to let the peace and quiet soothe her nerves, but all it took was a glimpse of the silk tie lying on the floor to rattle them again.

She picked it up, smoothing it between her fingers. Marcus must have dropped it and now it was a stark reminder of how impossible it was going to be to dismiss him from her life until this whole dreadful situation was sorted out. And the first step towards achieving that was to phone Eleanor.

She changed into jeans and a sweater then called to Drac as she set off for the village. It was a fair way over the cliff-top and by the time she reached it the sun was sliding into the sea, tinting the waves blood-red. Eden stopped outside the inn and drank in the view, arming herself with the beauty of the scene against the unpleasantness to come. But there was no putting off what had to be done, no matter how distasteful she might find it.

There were just a couple of fishermen in the bar when she went in. They nodded to her then carried on with their conversation, neither ignoring her nor rushing to draw her into their midst. Over the past year the villagers had come to accept her but she would always be considered an outsider compared to those who had been born and bred in the close-knit community.

Eden smiled at the man behind the bar. 'Is it all right if I use your phone, Harry? It is long-distance but I'll get the operator to reverse the charges.'

'Help yourself, Miss Moore. Oh, and before you go I've got something for you.' He placed an envelope on the counter, a faintly smug smile on his lined face. 'Had an American in here earlier on. He bought one of your paintings. I asked a bit more for it than you'd suggested, seeing as he was so keen.'

Eden opened the envelope and gasped as she drew out a healthy wad of notes. 'Harry, that's great! Which one was it?' She looked round, easily spotting the gap on the wall beside the snug door. 'That one of the village at sunset?'

'Aye. Really taken with it, he was. Asked no end of questions about you. Said he'd seen some of your work in some smart London gallery and made a point of stopping off here to meet you but you weren't in when he called at your place.'

'London?' Eden frowned. That seemed odd because as far as she knew none of her work had been bought by the city galleries. But then Harry could have got the facts wrong. She gave him a grateful smile and peeled some notes off the wad to hand them to him. 'Well, it's really marvellous. Thanks, Harry. Here you are.'

She had an arrangement with Harry, paying him a commission on every painting sold from the pub. It worked well and suited them both. Between the pub and her other outlet, an artist's co-operative in the nearby town, she made a comfortable living. In fact life had been extremely pleasant until last night when Marcus

Cole had turned up with his threats and accusations and turned everything upside-down!

Murmuring her thanks again, she slipped behind the bar and placed the call but the phone rang and rang unanswered. Eden replaced the receiver and went back into the bar and ordered a glass of shandy, but although she tried three more times there was no reply from Eleanor's number. Where on earth was she?

Where *was* Eleanor?

Eden chewed the end of the pencil, her open sketchpad momentarily forgotten as the question which had haunted her for the past ten days rose again. She'd lost track of the number of times she'd tried to get her sister by phone. She'd even written to her, but so far the letter had gone unanswered. She had toyed with the idea of travelling to London, but what was the point if Eleanor wasn't there? All she could think was that Eleanor must have gone away on holiday, but the sooner she came back the better as far as Eden was concerned!

Turning back to the sketch, she forced herself to concentrate, quickly outlining the rocks on the far side of the headland then drawing in the delicate lines of the yacht which was just sailing round it. It was a picture of contrasts, the jagged, forbidding rocks making the dancing yacht look so vulnerable. Soon Eden was lost in it, so that when a shadow fell over her she took her time looking up, then gasped when she found herself staring up at Marcus Cole. Her pencil skidded across the paper and she heard Marcus utter something under his breath yet she couldn't seem to find a reply. It took Drac's sudden arrival and the soaking he gave them both as he shook himself free of sea-water to snap her out of the trance.

She scrambled to her feet. 'Down, Drac. Sit!'

The dog sat, albeit reluctantly, quivering with a delight that Eden failed to share as he stared at the man who bent to pat him.

'Quite a welcome. Makes me glad I came.' Marcus glanced at Eden, one brow quirking. 'Well, almost.'

'What do you want?' She made no attempt to hide her hostility and saw him smile narrowly.

'It's a pity you can't learn from Drac how to greet visitors and make them welcome, Eden.'

She glared at him, ignoring the mocking rebuke. They both knew he wasn't welcome! Yet although she found it easy to ignore the taunt it was far more difficult to ignore the shudder which ran down her spine in response to the dark, disturbing tone of his voice, an odd little frisson which she bitterly resented. Marcus Cole represented a threat to both her and Eleanor's future, and that was the one thing she must never forget!

'You aren't welcome, so I can see no point in pretending otherwise. So, as I just said, what do you want?'

He bent and picked up her pad, studying the ruined picture. 'It's good, or would have been if I hadn't startled you.' He glanced back at her, a faint curiosity evident in his expression. 'Is this just a hobby or do you sell your work?'

She took the pad from him, folding the cover over the page. 'That is none of your business.'

'Oh, but it is. It is very much my business, the same as what I do is yours now.' He folded his arms across his chest and continued to study her. 'Surely it must have occurred to you that we will need to know a lot more about one another if we hope to convince everyone of our... relationship?'

Heat flowed up her cheeks at the choice of word. She turned away to pack her things into the canvas holdall, afraid of what he might see in her expression. She and Marcus didn't have a *relationship*! Threats and blackmail didn't add up to that! So why did her blood seem to heat, her heart start to pound when he spoke of it? It was very odd.

'Eden, Eden, surely you didn't think I would change my mind?' His laughter was deep and soft, full of taunting mockery and assurance that he would get his way.

She straightened up and glared at him. 'I hoped that you might see sense but obviously that was too much to expect!'

'If by "sense" you mean that I should let you off the hook this weekend, then yes, it was too much to expect.' He calmly took the bag from her and swung it over his shoulder, whistling to Drac as he started up the cliff-path.

Eden stared at his broad back open-mouthed, then rushed after him. 'I can carry my own things, thank you very much!'

He didn't pause, grey eyes glittering with an amusement which made heat curl in waves inside her as they lingered on her angry face. 'I'm sure you can. I'm sure you are completely liberated, Eden, but unfortunately I'm not. I was brought up to carry bags for the so-called weaker sex and it's a habit I find difficult to break.'

His long legs increased the gap between them as he carried on. Eden took a deep breath then started after him, calling him every uncomplimentary name she could think of under her breath, although with a man like Marcus there weren't enough of them in the dictionary!

She was panting by the time she reached the cliff-top. The path was steep and it hadn't helped that she had taken it at twice her usual speed. She stopped to draw air into her tortured lungs and could have wept when she spotted Marcus leaning indolently against the trunk of the gnarled spruce tree.

'I would have offered you a helping hand, only I thought you might consider it yet another insult.'

Eden stalked past him, closing her ears to the taunting laughter which carried in her wake. She opened the cottage door then glanced back at him, making no attempt to hide her reluctance. 'I suppose you'd better come in.'

'Thank you. You're too kind.' He followed her into the house and looked round with a small, almost wistful smile. 'I thought I must have imagined how peaceful this place is, but it seems I didn't. Have you lived here since you left London after your husband died?'

Eden carried on into the kitchen and took a jug of lemonade off the stone shelf in the larder. She didn't want to answer his questions about her past life but it seemed she had little choice. 'Have we time for a drink before the inquisition starts, Mr Cole? Or should I go and sit in a chair in the middle of the room while you grill me?'

His eyes narrowed at the stinging words but he merely shrugged. 'A drink sounds fine. I walked over from the village and it's quite a trek on a warm day like this. As for the questions, well, I'm sure we'll have plenty of time for them later.'

She wasn't sure she liked that answer; it seemed to suggest that this meeting was going to run on for some time. Didn't it bother him that she was openly hostile to his presence? Apparently not, because he looked totally at ease and not the least bit uncomfortable.

Filling a couple of glasses with the tangy liquid, she handed one to him without a word then carried hers outside and sat down on the step to drink it, leaving Marcus to join her or not as he chose. She stared across the bay, concentrating on the yacht, which was dropping anchor now, to keep her mind away from the tall, dark-haired man who seemed intent on upsetting her life. Yet when he came and sat beside her, stretching his long legs in front of him so that his thigh just brushed against hers, Eden gave up the pretence of indifference. Love him or hate him—as she did!—Marcus Cole was a man you couldn't ignore!

'It's a fantastic view. I can understand why you enjoy living here. Was it that which attracted you in the first place?'

Eden smiled thinly, swirling the lemonade around the glass in pale little eddies. 'When I found the cottage it was the middle of winter, there was a storm blowing and I couldn't see the view through the rain.'

'So what did make you decide to live here?'

'The fact that it seemed just about as far away from so-called civilisation and everyone who knew me! The view is merely a bonus. The real selling point for me was the cottage's seclusion. But I should have known that nothing perfect lasts forever. There is always someone just waiting to spoil it for you!'

Marcus's face set, his eyes turning glacial. 'You spoiled it for yourself. You moved back into that civilised society you claim to despise and moved back with a vengeance! You went after another woman's husband without a care for the fact that you could ruin her life.

So don't try blaming me for what you brought upon yourself!'

'Heaven forbid that you should ever bear the blame for anything, Marcus! I mean, you're so damned perfect in every respect, aren't you?'

He laughed with more than a hint of threat in the sound. 'I was hoping that we could conduct this meeting with a bit of decorum, but obviously that was too much to expect.'

'What could be decorous about blackmail?'

'About as much as there is about adultery. So what exactly do we have here? Two sins and two sinners? But I know which one I prefer to have committed!'

Eden struggled to her feet, her heart aching at the biting contempt in his voice, but he stopped her with a steely hand on her wrist. 'No. You're not going anywhere until I say you can. You're going to sit there and think about what you have done, all the damage you have caused. I doubt if you've ever given it any thought, have you?'

She'd thought of little else for days! In fact her head was reeling even now, which seemed a preferable reason for this dizziness rather than that it was his touch which was affecting her. 'You couldn't be more mistaken! Of course I've thought about it. I haven't stopped thinking about it since I left your flat!'

'But what exactly bothered you, Eden? Was it shame, or even guilt, for what you have done? Or were you more concerned about your own beautiful skin?'

He ran a fingertip lightly down her cheek, tracing the delicate curve of bone, the sensuous arch of her upper lip. 'You sit there without a trace of make-up on your face, looking as though butter wouldn't melt in your delectable mouth, but I know you for what you really are—a greedy, scheming woman who drove her husband to an early grave by her lust for other men, and who even now sees nothing wrong in what she does!'

'How dare you? You know nothing about my marriage—nothing!' She was shaking with anger yet it did little to quell the knifing pain she felt. 'You've based your opinion on lurid newspaper stories, that's all!'

He shook his head, the black hair falling in a heavy swath across his forehead before he pushed it back with an impatient hand. 'No, you're wrong. As a criminal lawyer I'm only too aware of what the papers will stoop to in their quest for a story, just how they will embroider the facts to suit their own ends. I've made my own enquiries about you, Eden, spoken to people who knew you and your husband, and it didn't take long to get the true picture.'

'What people? Geoff's friends and family?' She laughed harshly, the ugly sound of it surrounding them with a bitterness she'd thought she was over. But it wasn't over yet, not while Marcus used the past as a weapon against her. 'Oh, I think I can imagine the tales they told you. Something along the lines that I chased every man I met, that poor Geoff overlooked my little foibles because he loved me so much? That in the end he killed himself because I had broken his heart?'

'Are you saying that it isn't true, that all those people were lying?'

Scepticism hardened his voice and Eden looked away as unexpected tears stung her eyes. 'I'm not telling you anything. What's the point when you've judged me already on this *evidence* you've found?'

She shook his hand off and got up, walking unsteadily to the end of the garden where a white picket fence formed a barrier against the rocks below. She would be damned if she would cry in front of him! His cruel accusation had been no worse than all the others she'd had to bear after Geoff died, yet it seemed to hurt so much more. The tragic irony was that no one had deliberately lied. Geoff's friends and family had told the truth as they knew it, the truth as Geoff had made them believe it. He had been obsessively jealous during their marriage, accusing her time and again of having affairs with men she'd barely known, until in the end Eden had almost believed the accusations herself. It had taken his death and the gradual reawakening of her self-esteem to show her that she had nothing to feel guilty about.

'The evidence was based on my own findings, not just hearsay. And perhaps you can deny all those old stories, but can you deny that you and Rob have been having an affair?'

Suddenly Marcus was beside her, so close that Eden could feel the heat of his body against her wind-cooled flesh. She didn't dare glance at him, hearing the contempt in his voice as he levelled the question at her. The temptation to blurt out the truth was almost overwhelming but she had to remember Eleanor and why she was doing this. Yet to hear Marcus speak to her that way tore her apart. Why should it matter what he thought of her? She had no idea, but every harsh word left a fresh scar.

'Can you deny those photographs, Eden? Of course you can't!'

He damned her with the final bit of evidence, his voice dark with disdain. She turned her head away, almost blinded by tears as she stared out to sea, concentrating her whole attention on the yacht as though her life depended upon it. She could just make out a figure on the deck untying the dinghy and she stared at it so hard that her vision blurred, overwhelmed by the sheer futility of her situation once again.

Marcus swore roughly, catching her shoulder to swing her round to face him, his grey eyes burning. 'Damn you, Eden, what point is there in this—this charade? We both know what kind of woman you are!'

She gave a broken half-sob, her eyes brimming. 'You're wrong...wrong!'

'How? Tell me how I've made a mistake!' His fingers bit into her shoulders, a sudden tension about him as he stared at her. Eden caught her breath, wondering what had caused this sudden urgency that she sensed in him. It was almost as though he *wanted* her to prove that she wasn't what he thought her to be, but that was crazy! Marcus Cole hated her. That was the one single certainty in this whole crazy situation, yet the silence lengthened, the tension deepened and the temptation to tell him the truth and watch that contempt fade from his eyes became almost unbearable...

The sudden roar of an outboard engine cut through the silence and Eden jumped. Marcus let her go abruptly and stepped back, his face set and uncompromising once more.

'This isn't getting us anywhere. We're just going round in circles when what we should be discussing is the coming weekend.' He glanced at his watch. 'I shall pick you up at seven so be ready for then.'

He turned to leave but this time it was Eden who stopped him, although once he had halted she dropped her hand from his arm, feeling the burning imprint that his flesh had left on hers. She felt disorientated, her mind still trying to deal with what had just happened, that strange feeling that Marcus had wanted her to say something to convince him that she wasn't the woman he believed her to be. But when he turned to her, his eyes glacial, she knew at once that she had imagined it. Marcus had formed his opinion of her and he wasn't interested in changing his mind!

She drew a sharp little breath to stem the sudden surge of pain, her face very pale in the clear light. 'Wh-what are you talking about? Ready for what?'

He barely spared her a glance, impatience in every line of his body. 'Dinner, of course. I've booked a room at the village pub because I had the feeling this wasn't going to be straightforward. Nothing ever is around you, Eden. However, I'm sure it will prove beneficial to meet on neutral territory. It should help keep our discussion impersonal and to the point.'

She was horrified at the suggestion. 'I have no intention of having dinner with you!'

'I'm afraid you don't have a choice.' He bent towards her, staring coldly into her white face with no hint of compassion for her obvious distress. 'I can't say that dining with you is number one on my list of things I want to do. If I had my way, Eden, then I would make damned certain that our paths never crossed again. Unfortunately that isn't possible, so I shall pick you up at seven tonight and we shall have dinner and over dinner we'll try to get to know all the intimate little details of each other's lives.' He smiled slowly, deliberately taunting. 'Or in your case perhaps not *all*, just enough to convince Becky and everyone else that we know one another as lovers should.'

She was smarting from that last stinging gibe and glared at him. 'Even if I agreed to come, which I have no intention of doing, you don't imagine that we will fool anyone into believing that? You and I lovers...come on, Marcus!'

'Oh, they will believe it, my sweet. I'll make certain of it, no matter what lengths I have to go to!' He had her in his arms before she could gasp a protest, holding her to him as he smiled icily into her violet eyes. 'I don't intend that Becky should get hurt, no matter how objectionable I personally find the role I've been forced to play. Everyone will believe that you and I are as crazy for one another as that note you wrote implied.'

'You're mad! No one will believe it...especially not Rob!' She pushed against his chest but he just pulled her closer, trapping her hands between them, as he laughed into her angry face.

'Worried that he'll be so upset at seeing us together, he'll say something? I don't think so! I've made it plain to Rob what to expect if he tries to see you again. Oh, he might not like me calling the shots but he will do as he is told because he knows only too well that I mean every word I say. And by the end of the weekend Rob will be as convinced as everyone else that you and I are the perfect couple and that any hopes he might be harbouring about rekindling your affair at a later date are pointless.'

Perhaps it might have worked if she'd been Eleanor! Eden could only guess what Rob's reaction was going to be when he was confronted with her. It laid another minefield around the weekend, convincing her...if she'd needed convincing!...how impossible it all was.

'It won't make any difference if we swear on a bible that our relationship is the greatest love-affair since Adam met Eve! People will take one look at you and me together, Marcus, and immediately know the truth!'

'Think so?' He seemed to consider that, making her heart slow from its frantic tempo in relief.

'Yes. You know I'm right.'

'Then perhaps we should practise our roles, immerse ourselves in the parts we'll be playing to ensure that we're perfect when the time comes.'

Before she knew what was happening, he feathered his lips across her brow then let them glide down her cheek in a tantalising slide towards her mouth which made Eden's heart leap, although purely out of shock, she told herself.

'Stop that! What do you think you're doing?' She pushed as hard as she could to make him free her, feeling the steely strength of his body beneath the thin knit shirt he was wearing, the faint rasp of hair on his chest under her palms. In a sudden, intimate flash, a picture of him sitting in her living-room half dressed sprang to mind before she managed to blank it out and pushed again, even harder this time.

'What I'm doing is laying the groundwork, Eden. I think the technical term is method acting—living the part, in other words.' His voice held a note of cynical amusement, his mouth a disturbing, intimate threat as it slid on to hover at the very corner of hers.

'No! Marcus...please don't! Please!' She made no attempt to hide her distress, couldn't have done so even if she'd wanted to. Perhaps this was some sort of cruel game to him but suddenly she couldn't bear to have him play with her this way.

'What are you getting so upset about? I would have thought you'd be eager to capitalise on the opportunity this situation affords you.'

'I don't know what you mean. Let me go!'

She tried to free herself again but he held her fast, his strength so much greater than hers that it was impossible to break away. She could only stand there and watch the cynical smile which curved his mouth as he drew back and skimmed her body with a look which made her shudder.

'Come on, Eden. We both know the score—just how often you have used that delectable body of yours in the past to get what you want.' He shrugged so that the hard wall of his chest brushed the tips of her breasts, sensitising the nipples so that they pushed against the soft cotton of her T-shirt.

Eden gave a small moan of shame and denial. Marcus had made no secret of his contempt yet she still responded to his nearness in a way which shocked her. 'No!'

He arched a brow, unrelenting as he carried on. 'No meaning that you haven't done such a thing in the past, or no meaning that you have no intention of doing so in the future?'

He gave a sudden harsh laugh and let her go so abruptly that she staggered. 'As the former is well-documented fact and the latter highly improbable with your track record, you must forgive me if I don't believe you. However, a word of warning, Eden. I am not like Rob or any of your legion of past lovers. While I am willing to do everything in my power to make this weekend a success, I think you should realise that I cannot be swayed by your... charms. Quite frankly, a few minutes of sexual pleasure wouldn't be enough to make me change my opinion of you.'

'How dare you?' She was shaking so hard she could barely stand. 'I wouldn't sleep with you for any reason, Marcus Cole!'

'Not even to get yourself off the hook?' His eyes held a glittering contempt. 'We both know that's a lie. You would do it willingly if you thought it would serve a purpose. After all, what's one more man to add to the list?'

'I hate you,' she whispered hoarsely.

'I'm sure you do, however I won't lose any sleep over it. I shall see you tonight. Oh, and don't even think of standing me up, will you, Eden? You would only regret it.'

He turned and started along the path without a backward glance. Eden stared after him, trying to whip up her anger and use it to nullify the pain she felt. Maybe Marcus wasn't entirely to blame; those articles in the papers, the testimony of all those people who had known her and Geoff, this affair Eleanor had been having— they had all contributed to this picture he had of a woman with no morals and even less scruples. She could understand *how* he had made such a mistake but it didn't help ease this knifing pain she felt, this bitter, devastating, *irrational* hurt, that Marcus should look at the facts and fail to see beyond them to the truth.

CHAPTER FIVE

THE restaurant was busy as usual when they arrived that evening. The combination of good food and the tales Harry told of the wreckers who used to lure ships to their doom on the treacherous coastline ensured that the inn, although rather off the beaten tourist track, did a healthy trade.

Harry waved to them from the bar but was too busy dealing with customers to come across and speak to them. Eden was glad. Harry knew her better than anyone in the village and might notice there was something wrong. Oh, she had done her best, dressed with care in a deep blue silk dress, made up her face to disguise her pallor, but the outer appearance of normality was a sham. Inside she was raw and bleeding from the wounds Marcus had inflicted on her that afternoon.

Harry's daughter, Lisa, showed them to a table near one of the mullioned windows which overlooked the bay. It was obvious from the way Lisa smiled at Marcus that she found him attractive, and who could blame her? With his dark good looks and aura of sophistication he was enough to turn any young girl's head. But Eden knew what lay behind the smooth exterior, that black heart which beat inside his chest!

While Marcus ordered drinks she looked round the room, but the other diners were all strangers apart from a huge, blond-haired man sitting alone at a table near the door. There was something vaguely familiar about him which puzzled her as she couldn't recall where she had seen him before. It was only when he raised his glass to her in a laughing toast that Eden realised she'd been staring and hurriedly looked away, only to find her gaze tangling with Marcus's contemptuous one.

'Up to your old tricks already, Eden? My, but your broken heart must mend quickly if you're over Rob and on the look-out for fresh conquests so soon.' He bent closer, eyes glittering as he pinned her with a look of loathing. 'However, I'm afraid I shall have to curtail your plans at present. We need to concentrate on the coming weekend, not on your over-developed appetites!'

He wasn't jealous. Eden knew that as a certainty, but her emotions were already so raw that his tone and the words combined to open a wound which was barely healed. How many times had Geoff accused her of the same thing, berated her for intentions she'd never had? He had been obsessive when they were out, watching her like a hawk, weighing up each word and measuring each smile she gave until she'd been afraid to speak to any man in case it gave rise to another of their bitter confrontations.

Not that Geoff had ever shown his feelings to others, of course. On the surface he had always appeared the charming, witty man whom his friends had held in such esteem. Yet Eden had learned to dread the moment when they left the party or when the last guest departed from their house because then the mask would drop from him, jealousy turning his face into a travesty of the charming countenance he'd presented to the world.

He would lash her with his tongue, the cruel words raining down like blows, the vile accusations pouring from his lips to drown any protests she might make, until in the end Eden had learned not to make any. But now, when she was so vulnerable, the memories came rushing back, so that she could feel herself start to tremble.

'I...' The words wouldn't come, her throat locked on a spasm of helplessness at being accused so injustly again. Tears flooded her eyes so suddenly that she had no chance to blink them away. They spilled down her cheeks and she heard Marcus give a rough, faintly startled exclamation before he leant over and caught her hand.

'What is it? Are you ill?' He squeezed her hand, unconsciously rough now in his urgency. 'Eden...?'

'You...you're hurting me,' she whispered brokenly.

He looked down at their hands and relaxed his grip although he didn't free her. Almost without thought he smoothed the slender length of her fingers with his thumb. 'I'm sorry. I didn't mean to.'

'Didn't you?' She gave a hollow, broken laugh, looking down at their joined hands so that she missed the sudden flash of emotion which crossed his face. 'You've hurt me from the first moment we met, Marcus.'

His fingers tightened convulsively before he made an obvious effort to relax his grip, his voice grating when he finally spoke. 'I never set out to do so.'

'Forgive me if I find that hard to believe! I thought hurting me and making me pay for my sins was your *raison d'être*, Marcus! You certainly seem to derive pleasure from it.'

His eyes were suddenly glacial. 'All I ever wanted was to make sure that my sister didn't get hurt.'

'And that's your excuse for everything you've done?' Her voice had risen and suddenly she realised that they were starting to attract attention. She pulled her hand free and looked down as she toyed with the fringed ends of the linen place-mat. 'Can't you see that forcing me to go to your sister's house will hurt me, that it's madness to expect me to go through with such a crazy plan?'

'So that's what this is all about?' He sat back in his chair, a derisive half-smile curling his lips. 'You really are an accomplished actress, Eden. You almost had me fooled, and I've seen some good performances in my time in court. But I'm afraid your histrionics won't work. You are coming with me to Becky's and you are going to act your rotten, scheming little heart out, otherwise you will be giving your next performance for the benefit of the tabloids.'

He called Lisa over and gave his order, sitting back calmly while Eden asked for the same although she had no idea what it was. Her appetite had been ruined by what had just happened, by Marcus's absolute refusal to see her in any light other than the worst one possible. She glanced across at him, watching the way his face softened as he responded to something Lisa said, and felt her heart ache with a rare pain. Of all the injustices she'd suffered in her life, the fact that Marcus believed her capable of so many awful things seemed the worst.

'So that's just about it.' Marcus ticked off points on his long fingers. 'You're twenty-seven, you studied art in London, but were brought up in New Zealand until you were thirteen, which accounts for the reason why the papers were so short on background information about you. You are an only child and both your parents are dead. As for your marriage . . . well, I think we shall just bypass that.'

Eden put down her knife and fork and gave up all pretence of eating. Marcus had treated her like a hostile witness, firing question after question at her until she couldn't recall half the things she'd told him apart from that lie about being an only child. Now the thought of it made her feel sick.

When Lisa appeared to ask if they would like dessert, she refused, unable to eat another mouthful. Once the table was cleared and coffee poured, she concentrated on drinking it to steady her nerves yet still jumped when Marcus suddenly fired yet another question at her.

'Now are you sure you've told me it all?'

'What do you mean?' She set the cup down, suddenly afraid of spilling the coffee.

'There's nothing you've conveniently overlooked, no rattling skeletons I don't know about? Although what else you could have packed into an already hectic life I have no idea.'

If only he knew! Guilt was an icy finger trailing down her spine and she stemmed a shiver as she looked down at her cup. 'No. There—there's nothing else you need to know.'

'Mmm, that doesn't quite answer the question but I think I'll let it lie for now and rely on the fact that you know it would be a mistake not to tell me about anything which might cause problems.'

She laughed bitterly. 'I imagine who I am could be problem enough! Aren't you worried that Becky or one of her guests will recognise me this weekend, Marcus? I mean, does the idea of being linked to a woman like me appeal to you?'

He studied her in silence, grey eyes trailing slowly over each feature. 'Out of choice I would never get myself entangled with a woman like you, Eden. You're far too rich a taste for my palate in so many ways. However, needs must, and safeguarding Becky's happiness right now is far more important than my own feelings. As for people recognising you...' He shrugged, one brow lifting slightly as he continued to study her. 'I doubt that wil' happen. None of the pictures I've seen has done yo justice, my sweet little temptress. You're far more al luring in the flesh, with that beautiful skin, those in credible eyes. And no photograph could possibl reproduce that aura of innocence you possess. I ca understand how your poor husband and so many others including Rob, were taken in, even though I'm not foo enough to be misled by the packaging.'

He picked up his cup and took a sip of coffee. Ede drew a small shaky breath, trying to control the burnin pain at the double-edged compliment. He had neve made any attempt to disguise how he felt about her ye that didn't seem to soften each fresh insult. They hurt far more than they should in the circumstances, yet sh couldn't inure herself against their sting, it seemed.

'Now, is there anything else you feel you should know about me?'

She forced a carefree smile, refusing to let him se how much he had hurt her. 'I doubt it. Apart from seein your dental records I think I have the complete picture And I doubt anyone will grill me as you have done!'

His eyes narrowed, glittering twin slivers of grey ice 'I don't intend there to be any slip-ups. Understand And when you see Rob try to remember that it's the firs time you two are supposed to have met.' He smile coldly. 'No matter what intimate memories you share.

Eden looked away, assailed by a sudden wave of fear She had no idea what would happen when she did mee Rob! Did he know that Eleanor had been using her nam as an alias, or would it come as a shock to him?

Her troubled gaze unconsciously strayed to the blon man by the door and she felt her cheeks go pink whe he gave her a sympathetic smile. How ironic that he mus

believe that she and Marcus were having a lovers' tiff!
However, before she could become really uncomfortable
at the thought, the man stood up and laid some notes
beside his bill then strode unhurriedly from the
restaurant.

'Never mind, Eden. Another time, another man, I
expect. Living here in the wilds isn't as inhibiting to you
as I first imagined. You must have a steady stream of
fresh conquests passing by your door.'

Suddenly she couldn't stand Marcus's cruel taunts a
moment longer. She jumped to her feet and ran to the
door, uncaring what anyone thought. After the light in
the restaurant, the blackness of the night came as a surprise and she stumbled as she stepped down on to the
path and would have fallen if strong hands hadn't caught
her and set her firmly back on her feet.

'Careful, ma'am.'

The man's voice was gravelly and deep, his hands pol-
itely impersonal as he set her straight. Eden gave him a
strained little smile and moved away.

'Thank you. I didn't realise it was so dark. I missed
my footing.'

The man glanced towards the sky, his blond hair just
a pale impression. 'It sure is. Just like the sky back
home.'

Eden strove for composure, forcing a note of polite
interest into her voice. 'You're American, aren't you?'

The man gave a great booming laugh. 'I surely am!
And I don't suppose I could hide it even if I wanted to.'
He held his hand out. 'The name's Smith, Shiloh Smith.'

Eden shook his hand. 'I'm very pleased to meet you.
I'm Eden Moore.'

'Oh, I know who you are, ma'am.' He continued with
a broad smile when he saw her startled frown, 'I bought

one of your paintings the other day and Harry pointed you out when you came in tonight. I would have come over and introduced myself but...' He gave an expressive shrug and Eden drew her hand away, feeling embarrassed at what he'd witnessed.

'Well, it has been nice meeting you, Mr Smith. I hope you enjoy the painting.'

'I'm sure I will.' He glanced past her, a faintly speculative expression on his face. 'Are you sure you're all right now? It was obvious that you and your friend were having a bit of a quarrel back there and I know from experience just how upsetting they can be.'

Eden followed his gaze and sighed wistfully. 'It wasn't what you think.'

'No?'

She could sense his curiosity and suddenly, inexplicably, felt a need to tell someone about what was going on. 'No, I——'

The inn door suddenly opened, spilling light across the path, and she stopped abruptly as she saw Marcus coming out. Shiloh Smith glanced at him then nodded to her. 'Well, I guess I'd better be off now. Goodnight, Miss Moore. Take care.'

He walked down to the harbour and climbed into a dinghy moored against the wall, starting the outboard motor to head out towards the mouth of the bay and the yacht Eden had noticed earlier, thereby solving the mystery. He must be the man she'd noticed on deck earlier, so no wonder he had looked familiar.

'I have to give you full marks for perseverance, Eden. Nothing deters you, does it? No wonder you led your poor husband such a dance.'

Even hours of soul-searching later, Eden couldn't explain why she did it. One minute she was just standing there with Marcus's taunts raining down on her, the next her hand was arcing through the air to connect with his cheek in a stinging blow. The sound of it seemed to steal her ability to think or even move for a moment, then, with a cry of distress, she turned and fled; but she got no further than a couple of yards before Marcus caught her, his hands bruising as he hauled her to a halt, his eyes glittering with a fury which terrified her.

'You little hellcat! It's time someone taught you a lesson you won't forget.'

He dragged her to him, his eyes blazing as he took her mouth in a bruising kiss meant only to punish. Eden struggled wildly, hands flailing against his chest, but he merely captured her wrists and dragged her arms down behind her back so that her body was arched painfully into contact with his while he continued the punishing assault on her lips.

With a desperation fed by panic, Eden managed to drag her mouth away. 'No! Please, Marcus... not like this... please!'

It wasn't quite what she'd meant to say, the words taking on a subtly different meaning which Marcus seemed to interpret at once. He drew back, staring at her in a way which made a shaft of heat run through her body.

'If not in anger then how should I kiss you? Like this, Eden?' His mouth brushed over hers, feather-light and disturbing this time, sending heat surging along her veins in a shocking tide of sensation. He drew back slightly, eyes intent and glittering with something which made her even more frantic to escape him. 'Was that better?'

'I... No!'

He laughed deeply, smoothing her body against his as he bent towards her once more so that she could feel every hard line of his powerful legs against her own, the steely strength of his chest flattening her breasts. 'No? Then I shall have to try again. Maybe this is more to your liking?'

Suddenly, shockingly, she was on fire, wave after wave of heat licking along her veins, stemming from the point where their two mouths joined. Marcus was kissing her now with a passion she had never experienced before, his mouth expertly making its demands yet giving her back so much more.

Eden whimpered when she felt his tongue tracing the outline of her lips before delicately probing between them. She felt stunned, overwhelmed by sensation, her whole body throbbing heavily. When he slid his hands beneath the heavy weight of her hair and stroked the nape of her neck it was the most erotic stimulation she'd ever felt, unleasing inside her a desire she'd never experienced before.

Without conscious thought she responded to it, her arms lifting to link around Marcus's neck while she drew him closer and kissed him back, yet even as her fingers were sliding into his hair she felt her wrists being gripped and her arms being forced down by her sides.

'No, I don't think so. This has gone as far as I intend it to, although I suppose I should apologise if that has left you somewhat frustrated.'

He let her go, the cynicism in the smile he gave her sending ice sliding through her veins. He gave a low laugh which held no trace of amusement as his gaze lingered on her flushed face, the faintly swollen contours of her mouth. 'Such an ardent response would be flattering if I didn't know that it owes more to your over-developed libido than to my expertise.'

How could he do that? How could he stand there and say such cruel things? To the world at large, and to Marcus in particular, she was the very worst kind of woman, a tramp with no morals. And that was so far from the truth it was almost laughable.

She had been a virgin when she had married, clinging hold of her ideals that she would give only to her husband that gift. Yet it had been her very inexperience and Geoff's inability to arouse her passion which had laid the foundation for their disastrous marriage. He had lacked the patience to teach her about lovemaking then blamed her, accusing her of having other men to satisfy her needs until in the end anything she had ever felt for him had died under the relentless accusations. Passion had been unknown, untasted, until now in Marcus's arms! And now all he could do was stand there and taunt her with it.

Without a word, Eden turned and walked to the car, her movements automatic as some part of her mind untouched by the agony took over. When Marcus got in beside her and started the engine she looked out of the side-window, afraid of looking at him in case she broke down.

When he drew up outside the cottage, she got out still without speaking but he stopped her from closing the door as he leant across the seat. In the moonlight his face was a negative of light planes and dark shadows, his eyes silvery as they glittered up at her with an odd kind of anger.

'You asked for everything you got!'

'I apologise for hitting you,' she said flatly. 'It won't happen again.'

He swore as he flung his door open and got out. 'Too damned right it won't! Try that again, Eden, and you will be sorry, make no mistake!'

Her eyes rested on his angry face, holding a pain-filled bitterness she was unaware of. 'I'm sorry now. I couldn't be any sorrier, in fact.'

She started down the path, not pausing when he called her back, his tone rough yet seeming to hold a note which made her foolish heart ache. Eden closed her mind to the sound. It was just another trick, not a real apology. What was real was the simple fact that Marcus held her in total contempt.

The car roared away and she let herself in, seeing first to Drac before climbing the stairs to her room. Opening the window, she stood in front of it and let the sound of the sea beating the rocks below pound her senses. Time and tide waited upon no man, and the pain she felt now would dim and lose its potency as other painful experiences had done. She simply had to see this as yet another episode in her life to get through.

With a sigh, she unzipped her dress and went over to the wardrobe to put it away. Making space for the hanger on the rail, she heard a rustling of paper and, intrigued, she felt in the pocket of the black suit and pulled out a crumpled sheet of paper, and started reading it before her memory jarred to life.

Darling, I can hardly wait for this weekend to come, to be with you again and lie in your arms, hold you in mine for a few precious hours which will be ours alone to share...

Her eyes misted, her fingers crumpling the paper as she walked back to the window and rested her head against the frame to stare at the ceaseless swell of the ocean. They might be Eleanor's words but it was her name on the bottom of the note, her heart which cried out against the unfairness of it all. She could never condone what her sister had done but she envied her that fearless ability to love and be loved. What must it be like to want someone that way and know that he wanted you?

And if just fleetingly her thoughts touched on Marcus Cole and how it would feel to love and be loved by a man like him, then she immediately dismissed them. She could never love Marcus, and he most definitely would never love her!

There was a stiff wind blowing the next morning. Eden picked up the basket of washing and carried it outside to peg it on the line. The wind caught the flying ends of linen, blowing it up towards the sky, and Drac barked excitedly as he leapt up to catch it.

Eden quietened him then walked to the end of the garden, shading her eyes as she stared across the bay. The yacht was still lying at anchor, its sails furled although she could just make out Shiloh Smith on deck. He had made no mention of how long he intended staying in the area although he must have been around for some while now because Harry had told her about him buying the picture well over a week ago. It made her wonder what had kept him here before she shrugged it aside as none of her concern.

She'd half turned to go back to the house when the sound of a car drawing up on the road above brought her to a sudden stop. She had few visitors so it wasn't difficult to guess who it might be and suddenly she knew, as the memories of their last meeting came flooding back, that the last person she wanted to see right now was

Marcus. But it seemed she didn't have a choice as he appeared down the path.

He stopped when he caught sight of her standing poised as though ready to take flight, one dark brow lifting in a way which put her instantly on the defensive, a feeling heightened when he gave a softly provocative laugh.

'Now, I wonder why I get the feeling that you are less than pleased to see me?'

'Should I be pleased?' She stared back at him as the memories swelled inside her head to create a crescendo of images: the taste and feel of his mouth on hers, the power in his body, the cold, unconcealed disgust on his face afterwards... She took a sharp little breath to control the knifing pain. 'What do you want now, Marcus?'

'The only thing I ever wanted from you... to ensure that you make amends for this trouble you've caused.' He laughed harshly as he came closer. 'Believe me, you have nothing else which interests me, and I can say that in all honesty after having sampled what's on offer last night!'

'How can you? If you were any kind of a—a gentleman you wouldn't mention that!'

'And if you were any kind of a lady then you're right, I wouldn't. However, you aren't that, are you, my sweet little sinner?' His eyes skimmed her slender body in an open insult. 'Oh, I admit that you can *look* the part when you choose, but underneath is where it really counts and that's where you fail miserably.' He glanced past her and smiled in a way which sent chills down her spine. 'Ah, now I wonder if that is the reason why you were less than pleased to see me?'

'What are you talking about?' Eden glanced over her shoulder, still reeling from what he had said. Didn't he care how much it hurt to have him say such things? Apparently not, because he seemed intent on inflicting still more painful wounds.

'That.' He nodded towards the yacht, his eyes steely when they came back to her. 'Were you standing there hoping to lure Smith over here, like the sirens who used to lure sailors to them on to the rocks? Or maybe I'm being a bit slow on the uptake? Perhaps you already made arrangements last night for him to visit you?' He gave a harsh laugh which made her feel sick. 'Harry told me about him buying one of your paintings and how enthusiastic Smith was about your work. Seems you have a fan, Eden, although I'm sure it isn't news to you, the same as I'm sure that you've let him know how much you *appreciate* his opinion. Still, it does explain why I had the distinct impression that I'd come at an inconvenient time.'

He was so far from the truth that it would have been laughable in other circumstances, but not now, when each cutting word hurt. Eden forced herself to stand her ground, her face very pale, her eyes glittering with a pain she knew Marcus wouldn't see because he wasn't interested in her feelings. 'Any time you came would be inconvenient but I doubt you care.'

'You're right, I don't. I don't give a damn about what you do or whom you do it with...once this is over. Until then I am calling the shots, so if you've made any little liaisons with Smith then cancel them. After all, there's bound to be someone else along soon enough who can fill the gaps in your life.'

'I hate you, Marcus Cole!' Her voice was no more than a hoarse, pain-filled whisper but he was unmoved.

'Because I see you for what you are?'

'Because you're so blind that all you see is what you want to!'

'No. I see what's there, Eden. I'm not fooled by the packaging as so many others have been.' He pulled out his wallet and handed her a small card, the icy disdain in his voice cutting any further protest she might have made dead. 'That's my address, in case you've forgotten it. Be at my flat by six on Friday. And don't make the mistake of not turning up.' He shot another glance towards the yacht. 'I don't give a damn if it's Smith or a dozen others you lure here after this weekend but until this mess is sorted out you would be a fool to cross me, make no mistake of that! One way or another, I intend to see this through to the bitter end.'

He was gone within seconds, the throaty roar of the car engine echoing back at her like a chilling condemnation. Eden felt pain and anger and utter humiliation turn into outrage. How dared he speak to her that way? It was the final straw!

She hurried back inside the house and slammed the door, trembling as she stared around the room. Why, for two pins she would ring Marcus tonight when he'd got back and tell him the truth, all of it, just to have the satisfaction of hearing him admit that he'd been wrong!

The thought was so sweet that Eden savoured it for several delicious seconds as she walked to the dresser and laid Marcus's card down, smiling as she stared at the neatly printed letters spelling out his address. She could just imagine him picking up the phone, then his shock, his initial refusal to believe her, his final discomfort when he was forced to admit that he had made a mistake...

She frowned as she caught sight of the envelope almost hidden behind a jug then felt all sweet thoughts of revenge fade as she realised what it contained. She picked it up and drew out the photographs of her sister and Rob Lewis, staring at them with hollow eyes. They were a bitterly sharp reminder of what she could and couldn't do. If she told Marcus the truth then it wouldn't be she who suffered the brunt of his anger but Eleanor, and that was too high a price to pay for a moment's sweet revenge.

CHAPTER SIX

THE train was late getting into London so that it was nearer seven than six before Eden arrived at Marcus's flat. He opened the door to her, his face set. 'I thought I told you to be here by six?'

Eden stared back at him, feeling her own temper stirring to life. She'd spent a miserable journey worrying about the coming weekend and to be met with this was the last straw! 'If you have a complaint then I suggest you take it up with British Rail. I was on time, the train wasn't! Now, don't you think we should get on our way rather than stand here wasting time swapping pleasantries?'

His brows lowered. 'Before we set off I think I should make it plain that that sort of attitude won't get you anywhere. I don't intend that Becky should start doubting that this *relationship* of ours is anything but the real thing.'

He laid a heavily sarcastic emphasis on the words and Eden looked away from his cutting gaze, wishing she could find some way out of this whole miserable mess! Just for a moment a deep sense of resentment of Eleanor rose. Her sister had pulled a few wild stunts before, and several times Eden had had to sort out the problems she'd caused by her impulsive behaviour, but never anything as bad as this! When she saw Eleanor she was going to make it clear that nothing like this must ever happen again!

The drive was accomplished in a heavy silence which Eden made no attempt to break. She and Marcus had little common ground to ease conversation and banalities seemed out of the question. Yet when they drew up in front of the house Eden couldn't help but voice her admiration. Half timbered and of mellow brick, with the tall chimneys characteristic of the period when it was built, it was a testament to the love which had been lavished on its upkeep. Marcus had told her over that dinner that it had been in his family for centuries although it was Becky who made it her home now.

'It's beautiful. Don't you ever regret that you don't live here?' she asked impulsively as they parked in the driveway.

Marcus cut the engine, the last slanting rays of sun lighting his face as he glanced at her, emphasising the strong bones, that faint cleft in his chin. Eden experienced the oddest urge to run the tip of her finger down it and immediately curbed it. Marcus might be determined to make the right impression this weekend but the truth was that he loathed her and would loath her touching him even more. It was a deeply painful thought.

'Becky and I agreed it would be best that she live here when Mother moved to London. It would be both impractical and ridiculously self-indulgent for me to commute each day.'

Eden laughed, her fingers curled into her palms. 'Self-indulgent? You make it sound like a sin to do something you enjoy!'

'Personal pleasure isn't everything, although I doubt you would appreciate that.' His mouth thinned, his face suddenly harsh and condemning. 'Surprisingly enough, Eden, a lot of people have standards by which they live, standards they refuse to lower for either profit or pleasure.'

'Meaning, of course, that I don't?' She forced a smile, aching inside at yet another harsh assessment of her character. 'Yet surely you aren't accusing me of profiting from my affair with Rob?'

'Oh, I don't doubt that was purely for pleasure, but how about your husband? He was extremely wealthy, so was that why you overlooked the rather large age-gap and married him?'

It had been her mistake for getting into the conversation in the first place but it still hurt to hear him say such a thing. Without a word, Eden got out of the car, unable and unwilling to explain her reasons for marrying Geoff when Marcus couldn't give a damn about the truth. What would he say if she told him that she had married Geoff because he had seemed to offer her security when she had needed it most, that it had been his age and experience, not his money, which had attracted her? Of course she had been flattered by his interest; Geoff had been a highly cultured and charming man and any woman would have had her head turned when she had found herself on the receiving end of his attentions, but money had had no bearing on their relationship at all. Yet to tell Marcus that would be a waste of breath because he would never believe a word of it, and facing up to that stark fact hurt.

'There you are! I thought I heard a car.' Becky suddenly appeared round the side of the house, her arms full of flowers which she hastily deposited on the steps. Brushing aside Marcus's apologies, she linked her arms through both of theirs and drew them into the house. She looked far less strained than when Eden had last seen her, her pretty face free of the worry-lines. Eden didn't need to be told what had brought about the change and bit back a sigh. It seemed that everyone's future happiness was resting on her and it was a burden she wished whole-heartedly that she didn't have to shoulder!

'Rob's had to go out but he'll be back later. Now come along in and have a drink. Dinner will be half an hour yet.'

Well, that was some comfort at least! Eden had been dreading the meeting and was relieved that it would be put off although when she did finally come face to face with Rob Lewis she still wasn't sure how she was going to handle it.

Becky led them across a large oak-panelled hall into a room which had a comfortably lived-in look. Soft chintzes and faded rugs on the polished floor lent it an appeal which no amount of designer matching could ever compete with and Eden said as much to Becky, who smiled warmly.

'I know what you mean. It's my favourite room and I wouldn't change a thing.' She gave a forced little laugh, her smile fading. 'Even though Rob doesn't agree! He would throw most of the furniture out if he got half a chance.'

Eden said nothing because there didn't seem much to say which wouldn't sound critical. When Becky went to pour them drinks, she walked to the long window and stared out over the lawn which led down to a small lake. There was a pair of swans swimming regally across it and she watched them until Marcus suddenly joined her. He handed her a drink, his face grim and set so that for a moment Eden wondered what she had done, but this time it seemed she wasn't the one to have aroused his anger.

'God, but how I wish Becky had never got mixed up with Lewis in the first place! Even before I found out what you and he have been up to I wasn't over-fond of him. Becky had been on the verge of getting engaged to someone she had known since childhood, but then she met Lewis and that was that.'

Eden stared into her glass. 'She must have been in love with him. She still is, obviously.'

'And that's the reason why she's so blind to his faults?' He tossed back half of his own drink, his eyes glittering fiercely. 'And does that apply to you, Eden? Did you fall in love with him too?' He laughed harshly. 'Remembering that passionate little note you wrote, you definitely felt something, but love? No, somehow I can't quite see Rob pulling the wool over your eyes, my sweet. You have a lot more experience with men than Becky!'

'People cannot choose whom they fall in love with, not even you, Marcus!'

He had been openly insulting yet that bothered her less than his harsh assessment of the situation. She felt a sudden need to defend Eleanor's motives for pursuing the disastrous affair even while she could never condone them.

'And what is that supposed to mean precisely?' Marcus set his glass down and folded his arms.

Eden shrugged, suddenly wishing that she hadn't got herself embroiled in this sort of discussion. 'It doesn't matter.'

'Oh, but it does! If you have something you wish to say then don't be shy. After all, a couple as close as you and I are meant to be shouldn't have secrets.'

She glared into his mocking face, hating him for the continual taunts, that cold arrogance. 'All right, then. One day I hope you fall in love, Marcus. With someone

who isn't the perfect paragon you would like her to be!
I wonder what you'll do then? Will you end the relationship after coolly assessing its merits? Or will you
find perhaps that the heart can and does rule the head?'

'I suppose it could happen. Stranger things than that
have.' He appeared to give it some thought before he
smiled contemptuously. 'But I doubt it. So if you are
fostering any hopes along those lines, Eden, forget them.'

'I don't know what you mean.'

'No? Then let me make it plain. I might be able to
overlook a lot of things if and when I ever fall in love.
However, your past wouldn't be one of them.'

He moved away to refill his glass, laughing at some
comment Becky made. Eden turned to stare out of the
window, her eyes prickling with tears. Even without this
supposed relationship with Rob Lewis, Marcus's opinion
of her would be rock-bottom, thanks to what he had
read in the papers, and it was so unfair. She didn't want
Marcus of all people to believe those lies, yet why she
should feel that way she had no idea. Once this weekend
was over it was unlikely she would ever see him again
yet the thought that he would always think so badly of
her hurt bitterly. If there was one wish she could be
granted then it had to be that Marcus would one day
know the truth about her.

'Marcus! Oh, it really is wonderful to see you! I'm so
pleased you were able to come.'

Eden blinked back her tears and turned to see a
beautiful black-haired woman fling her arms around
Marcus's neck. He kissed her cheek, smiling at her with
such tenderness that Eden felt her heart ache. What
would it be like to have him look at her that way? It was
something she would never know.

'Eden, I'd like you to meet Natalie.'

Was that really *her* name said that way, all soft and warm? Eden's startled gaze flew to Marcus's face and lingered only for a second before she saw the icy disdain slide back as Natalie came across the room to greet her. He had merely been playing the role he'd adopted for this weekend and any warmth had been strictly for the benefit of their audience!

Her anger rose but she banked it down as Natalie spoke. 'I'm delighted to meet you, Eden. Becky has told me all about you and Marcus and...well, I'm just so pleased for you both!'

This was getting worse by the second, the lie drawing them all into its sticky web! Something of what she felt, this deep revulsion at tricking everyone, must have shown on her face because suddenly Marcus was there beside her, his fingers biting warningly into her shoulder as he slid his arm around her. He laughed as he feathered a kiss against her temple, his warm breath stirring her silky hair and sending an unwanted ripple of awareness through her. 'Eden is still a bit shy about it all. It does tend to knock one sideways!'

Natalie echoed his laughter. 'It certainly does! I don't think I've felt right ever since I met Flynn!' Her face glowed with happiness. 'Now I want to hear how you two met. I knew you'd been up to something recently, Marcus, when I had such difficulty tracking you down. Although if you had been at home then I might never have met Flynn, of course!'

She must have seen Eden's bewilderment because she elaborated. 'I left a message on Marcus's answering machine asking him to help me out with a problem I had and instead Flynn turned up and gave me more problems than I could list in a year! But the end result was worth it,' she added dreamily. 'But come on—tell Becky and me all the details! How did you two meet?'

'At a party.'

'In an art gallery.'

They both answered together then both stopped, leaving a small pregnant silence before Marcus said smoothly, 'What we meant was that we met at a party held in a gallery. Eden is an artist.'

'Really?' Becky joined them, smiling playfully at her brother. 'Marcus has been so very secretive that I know nothing at all about you, Eden. What sort of things do you paint?'

Eden forced a smile, feeling the tension in Marcus's body. He was worried about what she might say, and so he should be. This whole masquerade was madness! They were bound to trip up sooner or later and she knew who would bear the blame. 'Mainly seascapes of the Cornish coast where I live.'

'So that's where Marcus has been hiding himself away.'

Marcus smiled, running his fingertips down Eden's bare arm in a light caress which held a warning. Did he understand how she felt about the futility of what they were trying to do? Probably. He seemed to have a strange ability to understand her feelings! 'Eden has a cottage there, very remote and secluded, away from everyone and everything.'

He made it sound as though the cottage were their cosy little love-nest, which was so far from the truth that Eden felt a sudden need to jolt his self-assurance as hers had been jolted so many times since they had met!

'Mmm, once you close the door you're safe from the world and all its problems, isn't that right, darling?' She ran her hand lightly down his cheek and felt him flinch although with Natalie and Becky watching he didn't dare react as she knew he longed to. 'I always feel that the cottage is a haven where nothing *nasty* can intrude.'

His eyes were glacial when they met hers but his tone reflected nothing of his feelings. 'It is a very special place indeed.'

Becky sighed. 'It sounds lovely, although I don't know if I would like living somewhere so remote and far away from everyone.'

Marcus laughed deeply, sending a warning shiver racing through Eden. When she tried to draw away from him, he pulled her closer and held her there as he stared into her eyes. 'It isn't that lonely, is it, sweetheart? There are always visitors dropping by... for one reason and another.'

She knew exactly what he was alluding to all right, and her temper surged. 'Mmm, yes. It's amazing the number of people you meet in such an out-of-the-way place. I'm not sure if it's just the wonderful scenery which lures them there or what. Why, only the other day I met the most charming American who obviously finds something about the area deeply appealing.'

She laughed with playful amusement, feeling Marcus's body imprinting itself down the length of hers. Was he worried about what she might say? She hoped so because he was the one who had started it with his horrible insinuations! 'He even bought one of my paintings—a view of the village at sunset—as a memento, although I'm sure he won't forget his stay there.'

'It must be a lovely place. I hope you'll invite Rob and me down there some day——' Becky broke off as the telephone rang. She excused herself to answer it, closely followed by Natalie who said that she would go and check on dinner.

'What the hell do you think you're playing at?' Marcus made no attempt to hide his anger and Eden felt a momentary alarm as she saw the fury etched on his lean face before she quelled it.

She smiled sweetly at him. 'Playing at? I'm sorry but I don't follow you.'

He swore softly as he stared into her face with icy flames glittering in the depths of his eyes. 'I will not have you playing games, Eden. Understand? All those veiled allusions to Smith and the reason why he's been hanging around are to stop right now!'

'You were the one who started it!' She glared back at him, her slender body rigid with indignation. 'If anyone was making insinuations then look no further than the mirror to see the culprit, Marcus! Anyhow, I said nothing that wasn't true.'

'I'm sure you didn't.' His tone was contemptuous. 'I'm sure there's plenty to keep Smith interested but I doubt it's the scenery!' He skimmed her with a look of contempt. 'Men can soon tell when a woman is giving out the right signals and I'm sure you've been giving out plenty, Eden. He undoubtedly won't forget his stay there in a hurry, I'm sure!'

She'd meant only to pay him back in some small way but she should have known that in the end she would suffer more than Marcus ever would. She shook her head, turning her face away from that contemptuous gaze, aching inside with a bitter sadness. 'Shiloh Smith isn't interested in me. I...I don't know what he's doing in the area but it has nothing to do with me.'

'You really expect me to believe that?'

His tone told her what a mistake that would be. Eden shrugged. She knew what Marcus thought of her so all these constant reminders shouldn't be so intensely painful. 'That's up to you. You're the one who thinks he knows everything.'

'About you? Yes, I do. So save your breath. We both know that given half the chance Smith will be added to your list of admirers. It's just a pity that you've had to miss your chance this weekend.' His tone was scornful. 'Still, maybe he's keen enough to hang around a while longer. He must have money because that yacht is worth a packet so keep your fingers crossed that you've whetted his appetite just enough. It seems you might have latched on to a winner there.'

She swung round, eyes blazing, pain stirring her anger to life. 'I've already told you that Smith's being there has nothing to do with me but, as I said, it's up to you what you believe.' She smiled deliberately. 'If you find it . . . easier to carry on thinking of me in that way rather than admit to yourself that you might be wrong then go ahead.'

'Meaning?'

'That perhaps you're scared of facing up to the truth.' She gave a husky little laugh, wanting to hit back at him for all the heartache he was causing her and knowing the perfect way to do it. She moved closer and let her hands slide up his chest to rest on his shoulders, feeling the start he gave as every muscle tensed at her touch. 'Does it worry you, Marcus, that you don't like the idea of me with other men? Could it be that, despite everything, you aren't entirely . . . indifferent to me?'

Her hands curved around his neck, her fingers sliding into the cool dark hair at his nape while she stroked the rigid muscles. Marcus must be hating this, every second that she touched him, yet with Becky just outside the room he was powerless to make a scene. It was a small but infinitely sweet revenge for all the hurt he had inflicted on her!

He captured her hands and drew them down but made no attempt to push her away as she'd expected, just held her to him so that now she was the captive and he the captor while he smiled into her face with a searing contempt. 'I have never claimed to be indifferent to you. Far from it. I feel a whole lot of things when I look at you, Eden. Would you like me to tell you what they are?'

Suddenly, she didn't want to play this game any longer, didn't want to hear what he might say, each cold word which would inflict fresh wounds. She dragged her hands away but he merely caught her around the waist and held her so that he could look directly into her face.

'No! Marcus, I don't...!'

'Oh! Excuse me.' Becky stopped in the doorway and Eden felt colour run up her face as she imagined how it must look with her held so tightly in Marcus's arms. She had meant to pay him back but once again he had turned the tables on her, lending credence to the picture he was trying to paint this weekend!

He dropped a kiss on the tip of her nose then let her go as he looked over at his sister. 'Don't worry. I'm sure Eden and I can continue with what we were doing later! There's nothing wrong, is there?'

Becky forced a determined smile to her face. 'Not really. That was Rob on the phone. It seems he's been held up unexpectedly at a meeting so he might not get back tonight.'

Marcus's eyes narrowed. 'I didn't realise he was working on anything at present.'

'It only cropped up today, something urgent, I believe. I'm sure he'll tell you all about it.' Becky shrugged.

'You must know better than anyone how these things just turn up out of the blue. Oh, I know Rob holds only a very junior position in your chambers but you know how conscientious he is.' She gave a light laugh, which didn't quite hide the strain in her voice. 'Marcus is a slave-driver when he wants to be, Eden. I can't count the number of times that Rob has stayed back to finish some task or other just in case Marcus needs the information the following day! Still, we shall just have to carry on without him.'

She left the room, leaving behind a silence abruptly broken when Marcus laughed harshly. 'A couple of days ago I would have confidently said that you would know more than anybody about the amount of *extra* work Rob has been doing, but now I'm not so sure. Where do you think he is tonight, Eden? And who do you think he's with? Could it be that Rob has found someone to replace you?'

His voice dropped, edged with anger now. 'One way or another I'll find out and, believe me, Rob will regret it if he's decided not to heed my warnings!'

Eden stared after him as he left the room. Naturally she was relieved at not having to face Rob tonight but it was a relief tempered by fear. What would Marcus uncover if he started looking deeper into his brother-in-law's activities? She had no idea, just a feeling that if he ever found out how she had misled him then he wouldn't be pleased!

They had just finished dinner when a car drew up. Eden had found the meal an ordeal, the questions Natalie and Becky asked taxing her to the limit. Several times Marcus had smoothly intervened when she'd hesitated. He had appeared unruffled at maintaining the pretence but Eden knew that for her the weekend couldn't end fast enough!

Now hearing the car and suddenly wondering if it might be Rob after all made her heart run wild. But, mercifully, it turned out to be Flynn O'Rourke, Natalie's fiancé, arriving to take Marcus back to the village pub, where he was staying with his best man, for an impromptu stag-night.

Natalie made the introductions yet Eden sensed a certain coolness in O'Rourke's manner which she couldn't understand. On the surface he seemed charming enough but perhaps her awareness had been heightened by the situation she was in because she sensed an undercurrent to the polite conversation they had. But why? She had never met O'Rourke before so why did she have the feeling that he was weighing her up? Surely Marcus hadn't confided in him about this affair she'd supposedly had with Rob Lewis?

It was a bitterly unpalatable thought which stayed with her throughout the evening until she could cope with it no longer. She got up and excused herself, explaining that she had a headache and was going to go up to bed to sleep it off. Becky was instantly full of sympathy and insisted on showing her to her room, pausing for a moment in the doorway.

'I hope you feel better in the morning, Eden. Flynn's best man, Doyle, is bringing his wife over after breakfast so that we can go to church together. You'll like Gabrielle, I'm sure.' She gave Eden a quick hug. 'I'm really glad that you're here! Marcus works far too hard. He always has, ever since Father died. Father left a lot of debts and it was Marcus who saved the family from near penury. He nearly worked himself into the ground getting the chambers up to their present standing but the cost to himself has been enormous. He's had no real time for any serious relationships although women have come and gone in his life at a rate of knots! I did used to wonder if he and——' She stopped with a small, uncomfortable smile. 'Well, that doesn't matter now. I'm just so pleased that he has found you, Eden. It's obvious that you two are perfect for one another!'

Becky went back downstairs leaving Eden feeling worse than ever about the way they were deceiving her although Marcus's reasons for doing so were the best in the world. Wasn't she, too, doing this to ensure her own sister's happiness? It seemed they had that much in common although she doubted that Marcus would appreciate it!

She sighed heavily as she went into the bedroom and switched on the light to look round. It was a large room, furnished in keeping with the age of the house. Eden's gaze ran over the huge canopied bed with its cream and burgundy hangings, the age-darkened chests and robes, the pewter bowls of garden flowers, and felt some of her depression lift. It was like stepping back in history yet, when she explored further, the *en-suite* bathroom contained every luxury she could have asked for and was far too tempting to resist.

She filled the tub with scented water then got in, closing her eyes as she let the soothing heat flow through her tense body so that by the time she got out again and wrapped herself in a huge fluffy towel she felt more relaxed than she'd felt all evening. However, it took just one glimpse of the man sitting propped against the pillows in the bed to spoil it!

'What do you think you're doing? Get out of here at once!' Eden drew the towel around her, feeling heat invading every part of her body, as Marcus looked up. He set aside the book he'd been reading and raised one thick black brow.

'Why all the outrage? I should have thought it would be commonplace to find a man in your bed.'

Eden hung on to the towel, all too conscious of her nudity beneath its folds. 'When and if I ever find a man in my bed then it is because he has been invited! I didn't invite you, Marcus Cole. Now I am asking you once more what you think you're doing here.'

He eased himself up against the mound of pillows, drawing her attention to the fact that he wasn't wearing a pyjama-top. He had switched off the overhead light and now the soft glow from the rose-shaded lamps cast an intimate glow over the room. Sitting like that in the massive bed, his tanned skin even darker in the muted light, the shadowing of body hair visible across the muscular contours of his chest, he looked so *right* that Eden's heart gave a warning little flutter even before he answered.

'This is my room, Eden. So where else should I be at this time of the night?'

Eden stared helplessly at him then looked round, only then noticing the betraying evidence that he was telling the truth. She'd been so worked up before that she had never noticed the display of sporting trophies in a glass cabinet by the door, the row of framed certificates bearing Marcus's name. Now she wished she had been a little more astute in assessing the situation earlier.

'You can't stay here,' she said flatly. 'It's ridiculous even to think of it. We can't possibly... can't...'

It was incredibly difficult to voice the thought but Marcus appeared unperturbed, his tone silky smooth yet sending a frisson racing through her.

'Sleep together? But I thought that was what you were hoping might happen.'

'I... Of course not!'

He continued as though she had never spoken. 'I thought you were hoping I might succumb to your charms as so many men before me have done. You seemed to think it was a possibility earlier.' He laughed softly. 'And maybe I've decided to find out just what I've been missing.'

He held his hand out to her, his eyes grey and glittering, the colour of the pewter bowls. 'Want to show me, Eden?'

'No, I do not! We are not sharing that bed, Marcus. Let's get that perfectly clear!' She pushed the heavy weight of her wet hair back from her hot face and glared at him. 'If you won't find someplace else to sleep then I shall!'

'You won't.' His voice was suddenly harsh, the silky tones no more than a memory. 'Can you imagine what Becky will think if you start demanding a separate bedroom?'

'I don't care! I don't care what the whole world thinks, if you'd like to know. I am not sharing that bed with you!'

'Please yourself. It's your choice; just so long as Becky continues to believe that you and I are crazy about one another I really don't care.'

He picked up his book again, ignoring Eden as she hovered uncertainly in the middle of the room. She looked round uncertainly, her gaze stopping on the wingback chair by the desk, and sighed as she realised that would have to substitute for a bed.

Walking stiffly across the room, she hunted her gown and the marabou-trimmed robe from her case and carried

them into the bathroom, inwardly ruing her choice of
nightwear. It had been sheer impulse which had made
her opt for them instead of her usual oversized T-shirt,
something she deeply regretted now as she felt Marcus's
cool gaze following her as she came back out of the
bathroom. He probably saw the outfit as further evidence of her intention to seduce him! She hurried to the
chair and curled up, closing her eyes as he switched the
lights off.

'Goodnight, Eden; sleep well. And if it does get too
uncomfortable in that chair, remember this bed is big
enough for both of us!'

Eden closed her ears to the laughing taunt in Marcus's
deep voice, closed her mind to the picture he had made,
lying under the canopy, but she couldn't close her
traitorous imagination to what it might feel like lying in
his arms in the darkness...

CHAPTER SEVEN

THERE were pins and needles in her foot and aches and pains in every single muscle, it seemed!

Eden sat up and sighed. She was so tired, her eyes burning with the need to sleep, but sleep had proved impossible. Peering through the darkness, she could just make out the clock on the bedside table but couldn't read what time it said.

She got up quietly and crept across the room, biting back a groan. Three a.m.! She turned to go back to the chair then stopped, her heart thumping, when a large hand closed around her wrist.

Marcus rolled on to his side, propping himself up on his elbow as he glared up at her. 'Why don't you just get into bed and let us both get some sleep? I'm fast running out of patience listening to you rustling around in that damned chair!'

'No!' She tugged on her hand but he wouldn't release her. 'Please let me go!'

'So that you can keep us both awake for the rest of the night?' Anger hardened his deep voice. 'I could understand it if you were some trembling young virgin, but with your track record, sweetheart, it's verging on the ridiculous to keep this up. Just what do you imagine is going to happen if you get into this bed? Do you honestly believe that I'll be overwhelmed with lust?' He gave a harsh laugh. 'Perhaps we should just get it all over and done with, then maybe we can both get some sleep!'

With a speed which left her gasping he pulled her down on to the bed beside him and rolled her over, trapping her beneath his powerful body as he stared into her shocked face. 'Is this what you've been expecting, Eden? Or perhaps it was what you were *hoping* would happen? I would hate to disappoint you, whichever it is, and if it helps to put an end to all this wondering...'

His mouth found hers unerringly even in the darkness, relentless as he sought a response. Eden twisted her head on the pillow, trying desperately to evade him, but Marcus held her still as he ran his thumb over her mouth and parted her lips before bending to trace their outline with his tongue.

Heat seared her, wave upon wave of it, burning up from the depths of her body, shocking her with its speed and ferocity. Marcus touched her and she went up in flames, and that truly should shock her!

When he drew back she whimpered a helpless denial both of what she was feeling and what he was doing but he misunderstood. 'Don't you want me to stop now, sweet? Are you admitting to your needs at last?' He laughed softly, the deep sound sending an unwanted shiver running through the heat inside her. 'After all, I put a stop to your plans for Smith, so maybe you're feeling just a shade frustrated at being denied what you so obviously need.'

He ran his hand down her body then let it smooth back up to linger against the rigid hardness of her nipples, which were thrusting through the thin silk gown and robe. 'Your response would be flattering if it weren't for the fact that I know your body is highly tuned to give the response any man would appreciate.'

The heat disappeared to be replaced by a numbing cold which settled deep into her heart. Marcus considered her to be a tramp, a woman who would respond to any man's advances. If only he knew the truth—that it was his touch which aroused her so, no one else's! But perhaps it was better that he should never know so that he couldn't use it against her.

'Let me go, Marcus. If you don't I shall scream my head off, and I'm sure you can imagine what Becky might make of that.'

Her voice was flat, betraying nothing of the heartache and pain which seemed to be clawing at her insides. When Marcus made no move to let her go she stared back at him, determined to make him understand that she meant what she said, yet even as her eyes locked with his she could feel the fire start to flicker inside her again and was filled with shame. It seemed that even insults weren't enough to damp down this unexpected passion he could arouse in her.

She closed her eyes on a wave of humiliation and felt him roll away from her as he said flatly, 'I'm sure I can. And I'm sure that you can imagine what my reaction would be. So I suggest you think very carefully before starting something you would regret.'

He rolled on to his side, facing away from her. Eden took a slow breath and huddled beneath the blanket but its warmth didn't ease the numbing cold from her body, a cold which did not stem from fear. Marcus wouldn't touch her again. He'd only done so just now to impress upon her how much he disliked her. To Marcus she was beneath contempt!

Suddenly she couldn't stand it a second longer; the need to tell him the truth was irresistible. 'Marcus, I must——'

'Go to sleep. I really don't want to listen to anything you have to say right now.'

There was such finality in his tone that she fell silent. She stared up at the canopy and blinked back the hot tears. She wouldn't cry. She wouldn't shed one tear for a man who disliked her so much.

It was raining when Eden awoke. She lay in bed listening to the soft spattering of raindrops on the window, trying to summon up enough enthusiasm to get up and face what the day might bring.

She glanced at the other pillow, and the faint impression left there by Marcus's head. He'd got up just as dawn broke, moving quietly around the room, but she'd been awake. She hadn't slept at all until that point, but once he'd left she had fallen into an uneasy doze which had been filled with images she didn't want to remember now. Marcus had figured strongly in those dreams but she didn't want to recall the role he had played.

She sat up and gathered the long strands of her hair together to plait it, then shot a startled look at the door as it suddenly opened and Marcus appeared, a loaded breakfast tray in his hands. He carried it across to the bed and set it down on her lap, smiling cynically at her startled expression. 'Becky seemed to think that breakfast in bed would be the perfect conclusion to a romantic night in this four-poster.'

Eden flushed crimson, looking anywhere but at his taunting face. 'It's a shame you couldn't put her straight.'

'What, and ruin all her lovely dreams?' He laughed harshly as he walked over to the window and pushed back the curtains before glancing back at her with a slight lift of his brows. 'My sister is hoping for great things from this weekend, it appears.'

'What sort of things?'

'Oh, something along the lines that we shall announce our intention of following Natalie and Flynn to the altar pretty soon. Despite being married to Rob, Becky is an incurable romantic.'

'You make that sound like a crime.' Eden poured herself some coffee and watched him over the rim of the cup, trying to still the shudders her heart was giving, as though that taunting remark about their marrying had disturbed its rhythm.

Marcus smiled narrowly. 'Romance is superfluous in today's world. It achieves nothing, merely clouds the issue nine times out of ten.'

'And the great Marcus Cole would never allow his mind to be clouded!' she taunted. 'But there is one thing which does intrigue me, and that's how you intend to explain the sudden demise of this wonderful relationship of ours. After all, you're intent on convincing Becky this is the greatest love-affair since Antony met Cleopatra, so what are you going to tell her when it suddenly ends?'

'I suppose I could simply opt for a variation of the truth?' He came to stand beside the bed, staring down at her in a way which made Eden suddenly conscious of the thinness of her clothing. Last night in the dark it hadn't seemed to matter but now it felt as though he could see right through the thin silk to her nakedness beneath!

She drew the sheet up higher, but stopped when she saw the amusement in his eyes. Deliberately she let her gaze roam over him, taking stock of the well-washed jeans which clung to every powerful line of his thighs, the thin grey sweatshirt which emphasised the width of his chest and shoulders, and felt her pulse leap in a reaction she didn't want to feel.

She looked away, shaken by that swift flare of awareness, only to start nervously when Marcus sat down on the side of the bed, depressing it so that she slid towards him.

'Would you like to know exactly what I intend to tell Becky, my sweet little deceiver?'

There was a deliberate taunt in his voice and Eden lifted the coffee-cup to her lips and took a sip, forcing it down through a knot of pain and apprehension.

'Not really. Once this weekend is over we won't meet again, so what does it matter? Still, I would hate to spoil your fun, and I can see that you're dying to tell me, so...?'

He didn't like that; she could tell by the steely glitter in his eyes, feel it in his touch as he reached over and took the cup from her then tilted her chin so that he could look straight into her eyes.

'I could tell Becky that I found out you'd been having an affair with another woman's husband so decided you weren't the woman I wanted to share my life with. As I said, it would be only the smallest variation of the truth, wouldn't it?'

'Damn you, Marcus! You would really do it, wouldn't you? Blacken me in Becky's eyes out of... of spite!'

He shrugged, seemingly unperturbed by her outrage. 'Why should it worry you what Becky thinks? You weren't worried when you started your miserable affair with her husband.' He stood up and stared icily down at her. 'Perhaps this will teach you to choose your bedmates with a little more care in future.'

He left the room. Eden picked up a pillow and flung it at the door but it was a futile gesture. Marcus hit her time after time with the heaviest of blows and all she could retaliate with was feathers!

The rain stopped a few minutes before they left for the church. Natalie looked a picture in a calf-length silk organdie dress with white blossoms in her hair. Eden had chosen to wear the blue silk again, twisting a lemon and rose silk scarf at the neckline, and with her hair in a French-pleat she looked cool and elegant as she came down the stairs.

There was a small group of people gathered in the hall. Gabrielle, wife of Flynn's best man, Doyle, she had met earlier and liked immediately for her warmth and charm. Now Becky hurried to introduce her to the newcomers, who turned out to be a neighbour, Daniel Faramond, and his two young daughters who were acting as flower-girls at the wedding. A quietly spoken man, he had a way of listening intently to everything that was said, especially when Becky was speaking. Eden remarked on it to Natalie as Becky hurried off to answer the telephone and received a wry smile in return.

'Daniel has been mad about Becky since we were all at school together. They were on the verge of announcing their engagement when she met Rob Lewis at a party and fell for him. Daniel was devastated at the time but we all thought he'd got over it when he married Jill—that's his late wife,' she added in explanation. 'She died over a year ago. However, I sometimes wonder if he doesn't still harbour feelings for Becky when I see them together.'

How sad, Eden thought. Becky's life would have been so different if she hadn't met and married Rob Lewis, but then no one could choose whom they would fall in love with. Her gaze slid on, drawn irresistibly to where Marcus was standing, tall and elegant in his dark suit and white shirt. What would it be like to fall in love with

Marcus and know that he loved you too? It would be very special.

The thought slid into her mind so unexpectedly that when Marcus suddenly turned and looked straight at her she couldn't look away, held by something in his eyes, a host of emotions she couldn't begin to understand but which left her feeling breathless and shaken, as though she was verging on a discovery so mind-blowing that it threatened her whole world. Then, with an abruptness which left her bereft, he turned away just as Becky came back.

'I'm afraid there will have to be a change to our arrangements.' She drew a quick breath and forced a smile to her strained face. 'Rob has been held up and won't make it back in time for the wedding. As he has our car, it's going to create a problem getting everyone to the church, not to mention the fact that he was giving Natalie away.'

'Don't worry, Becky. I can take you, Eden and Gabrielle in my car.' Daniel stepped forward, looking concerned as he studied Becky's white face.

'Are you sure?' she asked tremulously.

'Of course I am. It will be my pleasure to help out.' Daniel's voice was full of warmth and some of Becky's pallor faded as she gave him a grateful smile.

'Thank you, Daniel.' She turned to Marcus, her expression unconsciously pleading. 'Would you mind standing in for Rob and giving Natalie away? It's really too bad of him to let everyone down like this but he said he couldn't help it.'

Eden watched the expressions chase across Marcus's face, understanding all too clearly what was causing them. He was furious with Rob, although obviously there

was nothing in his voice to betray that when he replied.
'Of course. As long as Natalie has no objections.'

Natalie smiled as she crossed the hall and laid her hand
on his arm. 'I can't think of anything I would like more.
I would have asked you in the first place but you'd mys-
teriously disappeared and Flynn and I couldn't wait to
get married any longer than was absolutely necessary!'

An oddly intimate look passed between them which
puzzled Eden. Natalie was crazy about Flynn but there
was obviously a deep empathy between her and Marcus.
Had they been at some point in the past more than
friends? Had Marcus once been in love with Natalie?

The idea was disturbing and bitterly painful yet Eden
couldn't understand why it should affect her so deeply.
Why should it matter to her whom Marcus had loved
or, indeed, might love in the future? She wanted him
out of her life as soon as possible! What he did was none
of her concern . . . was it?

The village church was full of flowers. Becky had dec-
orated it, using flowers from her own garden, and the
massive stone urns full of blossoms added to the time-
less beauty of the old building.

Eden took her place with the others and watched
Natalie walk down the aisle on Marcus's arm. Her face
was glowing with love as she made her way towards Flynn
and Eden felt a lump form in her throat. As they passed
the end of the pew where she was sitting, Marcus suddenly turned his head and looked at Eden, his eyes coldly
condemning. She looked away, holding back the bitter,
painful tears. That look had been a testament to everything Marcus felt about her, made more poignant and
painful by the occasion. Here was a woman setting out
on married life full of expectations, and there was she,

the woman who, so he believed, had tried to wreck another's happiness. How he must hate her, and how it
hurt to know it!

Laughter filtered into the garden through the open
window. Eden glanced into the room, feeling strangely
detached from the scene. The wedding had gone
smoothly and she had played her part yet she'd felt one
step removed from what had gone on.

Taking a sip of the champagne in her glass, she turned
her back on the merry-making and walked down the steps
on to the lawn, feeling the heels of her shoes sinking
into the damp grass. The sun was starting to slide behind
a bank of clouds, a warning that there was more rain
on the way, but Eden chose not to heed the darkening
sky as she stopped on the bank of the lake and watched
the swans making their regal progress.

Marcus had said no more than a dozen words to her
since they had got back from the church, and then only
because he'd been unable to avoid doing so. Was he
finding this self-imposed role difficult to play? Perhaps
she should feel glad if that was the case, but all she really
felt was this aching sadness, which had stayed with her
ever since Marcus had looked at her in church with every
bit of the contempt he felt showing on his face.

She drained the last of the sparkling wine then let the
glass dangle from her fingers so that a few drops fell on
to the grass by her feet and caught there like the tears
which clung to her lashes. She wiped them away with
the back of her hand but more appeared and suddenly
it seemed too much effort to wipe them away too.

'Why are you crying?'

His voice was so quiet that it didn't shock her and Eden answered the question without thinking. 'Because you hate me.'

'Can you blame me?' He came to stand beside her, staring not at her but at the swans, yet he saw the way she flinched and his expression hardened as though in anger. 'You didn't give a damn who got hurt. So why should I care if it hurts you to know what I think of you?'

Eden blinked hard to hold back the tears, shivering as the wind blew into her face, cold now that the sun had gone in. She turned abruptly to go back to the house, chilled not just by the drop in temperature but by Marcus's attitude and the sheer futility of pursuing this conversation, but he swung her back to face him.

He ran a finger across her lashes. 'Tears, Eden? But what for? Remorse, or because you don't enjoy the repercussions of what you've done?'

'I haven't done anything!' she cried, then repeated it in the desperate and probably vain hope that he might see the truth for himself. 'I haven't, Marcus.'

He let her go, his face unreadable, his voice devoid of all emotion. 'I think we'd better go inside before it rains.'

As though to endorse that possibility, heavy drops fell from the sky. Marcus turned back to the house but suddenly Eden knew she couldn't stand this a moment longer. She had to tell him the truth!

She caught his arm to stop him from walking away then gave a small cry when her feet skidded from under her on the slippery grass. Marcus reacted immediately, his hands encircling her waist as he caught her and steadied her against him. Under her palms Eden could feel the steady, measured beat of his heart, a beat which seemed to pulse from him to her until the air between them throbbed with its rhythm.

She licked her suddenly parched mouth and looked up to find his eyes locked on the movement of her tongue, silvery flames burning in their depths which both excited and scared her. 'Marcus, I...'

His hands tightened until they bruised her as he shook his head. 'Don't! Not one word. I don't give a damn what you have to say, what lies or excuses... I don't give a damn about anything except this!'

His mouth was hard when it took hers but there was no desire to punish in the pressure of his lips. He kissed her with a burning, abandoned passion which shocked her to the core. This was Marcus kissing her as though he had no intention or desire ever to let her go again!

She must have made some faint murmur of disbelief because the bruising pressure eased. Now the kiss didn't demand but sought a response, his lips moving mobilely over hers with an ardour she found impossible to resist. He wanted her to respond to the passion he was showing her and Eden was powerless to refuse as his tongue slid between her lips and enticed hers into a rhythm which made the blood surge along her veins like hot wine.

'Marcus!'

His name was a small betrayal of how she felt, this swirling mix of wild emotions which both shocked and excited her. He tensed at once, drawing her to him, smoothing his hand down her spine as he moulded her against his powerful length in a blatant admission of what he wanted from her now.

When his hand moved to cup her breast through the thin silk, Eden moaned sharply, her body responsive to the touch of his fingers, her breast growing heavy and full, the nipple rigid. Rain was spilling from the sky now, cold as it fell on them, but it couldn't quench the fire which was raging through her.

When Marcus lifted her she gave a startled gasp which turned into a moan as his mouth fastened over her breast while his tongue stroked her nipple through the clinging silk. She drove her fingers into his wet hair, holding his head to her as the waves of desire surged to a huge crescendo of need.

When he finally raised his head and let her slide to the ground there was both triumph and passion in his eyes as they focused on her face, her heavy violet eyes half closed with desire, her mouth red and swollen from the kisses they had shared. 'We don't need words, Eden, not when we can say so much like this.'

He drew her into the cradle of his hips, letting her feel the unmistakable hardness of his desire, and kissed her again, long and deeply, then let her go and held his hand out to her. 'Don't you think it's way past time we got this sorted out between us?'

For a moment fear of the mistake she could be making overwhelmed her, before she reached out and slid her hand into his without a word, knowing in her heart that this might be the only way ever to make Marcus start to see that he had made a mistake. Talking had achieved nothing because he had closed his mind to words, but could he close his heart to what they seemed to share, this wild passion? Surely once Marcus had made love to her, he would *know* she couldn't be the woman he believed her to be?

They walked back to the house in silence, stopping several times to kiss when the passion became too great to withstand. Marcus led her in through the back door, kissing her hard and fiercely as he backed her up against it and trapped her there with the power of his body.

Eden ran her hands down his back under his damp jacket, feeling the heat beneath his thin shirt, the faint tremor his muscles gave as her fingers smoothed over them, and the very last of her reservations disappeared. Marcus wanted her, and that was the first vital step towards understanding.

'Well, well, and what have we here? Seems I might just have done you a favour, then, brother-in-law.'

The man's voice broke them apart so abruptly that Eden had to draw in a shuddering breath as her senses whirled. She looked past Marcus to the man standing in the doorway and felt her heart lurch. She'd never met him before but she knew him, didn't need Marcus's curt greeting to warn her who he was.

'I see you finally made it, then, Rob. Where the hell have you been, or is that a silly question?'

'Didn't Becky tell you? I got held up trying to sort out a few problems with the Baxter case. But don't tell me you've missed me, Marcus, when you've had such delightful and entertaining company!' Rob laughed softly, almost vindictively, his handsome face set into a practised smile as he came further into the room.

Eden took a shuddering breath, filled with a heady mixture of apprehension and relief. She'd tried to work out what might happen when she and Rob met, how to cover up the fact that she wasn't Eleanor, but that no longer mattered because now she wanted Marcus to know the truth!

Rob Lewis took the last couple of steps just as Marcus moved aside and Eden steeled herself for what he would say but nothing could have prepared her for what happened.

'Eden, darling, you're looking lovelier than ever.' Rob's gaze skimmed her body in the clinging wet silk

dress before he bent and kissed her slowly on the mouth.
He drew back, smiling into her shocked face. 'And even
more alluring. Makes me regret ever giving in to Marcus's
threats.'

Eden stared at the man before her as she tried to find
something to say, words which seemed to be lost in some
deep pit in her mind. Then slowly her shocked gaze slid
past him to Marcus and she felt her heart break as she
saw the expression on his face. She had no idea what
Rob Lewis was up to but she did know that Marcus would
never believe her now if she tried to tell him the truth!

CHAPTER EIGHT

WHAT was going on?

The question spun endlessly through her head as they drove but Eden could find no answer to it, as she'd failed to find one all afternoon.

She went back over everything that had happened since Rob Lewis had greeted her in the kitchen, carefully blanking out the pain as she remembered the expression on Marcus's face. He had hardly said a word to her since then, merely informed her that they would leave once Natalie and Flynn did. When Becky had begged him to stay and drive back in the morning, he had been almost curt in his refusal. Marcus clearly wanted to end this whole episode, but how could it end when there was still the unanswered question of why Rob Lewis had pretended to recognise her?

Eden had tried several times to speak to Rob alone but each time he had evaded her, a faintly malicious amusement on his face. Obviously he knew what Eleanor had done, so was he merely playing along to protect her sister? Eden found that hard to accept because he didn't strike her as the kind of man who would worry about anyone but himself!

'Do you want to stop for something to eat? There's a service station coming up soon.'

Marcus's voice crackled with ice, the look he spared her just as cold. Eden swallowed down the stabbing pain and shook her head, trying not to recall what had hap-

pened between them by the lake such a short time
before . . .

'Then we may as well carry on.' He eased the powerful
car around a tight bend then picked up speed until the
hedges became just a green blur. 'We should make it to
your place before midnight, with a bit of luck.'

'The cottage? But I thought the plan was that we would
return to London and I would catch a train home?'

He smiled coldly. 'I prefer to know that you're safely
out of harm's way. The coast is just that bit further from
Rob, less of a temptation than letting you loose in
London. You surely didn't think that I missed all those
lingering looks you were giving him?' He laughed
harshly, his tone brutal now. 'It's over, my sweet little
temptress. Get that into your head and don't make the
mistake of thinking I won't carry out my threats. I only
hope that Rob hasn't, but that's something I intend to
check up on when I get back.' He cast her a coolly
mocking look. 'Would you like to know the results,
sweet, or would you prefer not to know if you've been
replaced in Rob's affections already, although you
haven't been slow off the mark in that respect yourself?'

'Is this how you get your kicks, Marcus? Do you enjoy
watching people dancing to your tune?' She was trembling, tension drawing her nerves so tight that she felt
sick.

'It doesn't give me any pleasure. I would prefer not
to have been drawn into this sordid affair, but Becky's
happiness is all-important, although if Rob has been fool
enough not to heed my warnings I can't guarantee that
it won't all come out this time.'

He shot her a quick glance, grey eyes glacial as they
rested on her, before he turned his attention back to the
road. 'You and Rob are well-matched. The main concern

of both of you is your own wants, your own needs.' His
voice dropped an octave, a cruel edge to the deep tones
which cut into her. 'Your desires.'

She turned away, holding back a sob. She knew what
he was alluding to, of course. He was using that moment
of passion they had shared as a means to punish her.
He had hated her before that and now must hate her
even more because he had been tempted to act in a way
he bitterly regretted!

The drive seemed endless despite the fact that Marcus
kept the car at the speed limit all the way. When he drew
up at the top of the path, Eden opened the door and
got out without a word, only turning when she heard
footsteps behind her. She kept her face carefully devoid
of all expression as she held her hand out to him and
fixed a mocking smile to her numb lips.

'So that's it. I don't imagine that we shall run into
one another in the future, do you?'

He ignored her hand, pushing his hair back as the
wind, tearing along the top of the cliffs, blew it across
his forehead. There was a full moon shining, so that
Eden had no difficulty in seeing the contempt on his
face. 'I hope not. So long as you remember to steer clear
of Rob, you'll save yourself any further problems.'

He moved to the rear of the car and lifted her case
from the boot. Eden took it yet didn't start down the
path immediately. Marcus would leave here still thinking
the worst of her and suddenly she knew that even if he
didn't believe her she had to try to explain.

'Marcus, I——'

'Goodbye.' He turned and climbed into the car,
starting the engine with a throaty roar which drowned
out anything she might have said. Eden watched it go
until its red tail-lights were mere pin-pricks in the night,

then slowly made her way down to the cottage, telling herself that it was for the best. She'd got this far, protected Eleanor—she shouldn't feel so desperately sad and bereft!

She slid the key into the lock, wishing that Drac were inside to welcome her home but she'd left him at the pub with Harry. She would collect him tomorrow but for tonight she would have to put up with being alone...

All further thoughts spun away as she pushed the door open. Moonlight poured into the cottage, lighting the scene of devastation. For a stunned moment Eden just stood and stared at the wreckage of what had been her home, then slowly set the case down at her feet and walked inside, her actions automatic as she lit the oil-lamps and looked round in disbelief.

From the pictures wrenched from the walls to the broken drawers of the dresser, the whole place had been systematically trashed. Broken china littered the floor along with pages ripped from her sketchpad. Numbly she bent to pick up a page, smoothing it between her shaking fingers as though she could wipe away the creases, the evidence of such mindless vandalism.

'You left your bag in... What the hell has been going on here?'

Marcus's voice mirrored her shocked disbelief. When she turned to stare blankly at him, he uttered a rough oath and came to her, his touch surprisingly gentle as he led her to a chair and swiftly righted it before sitting her down.

'Have you anything to drink in this place?'

She stared up at him, face paper-white, eyes almost black. 'Drink?' she queried uncomprehendingly.

'Whisky...brandy...anything like that?' He took her ice-cold hands between his own and chafed them gently. 'You've had a shock, Eden.'

'I...' She shook her head, looking away from his solicitous gaze which made her want to cry. Marcus was merely acting as he would with anyone in similar circumstances, but his kindness was almost too much to bear. 'I don't keep any here.' She laughed hollowly then felt the laughter grow until it filled the room. 'The one sin I don't need to own up to is drinking!'

He shook her hard, not roughly but with enough force to make the laughter die abruptly. 'Stop it! I'll make you some tea or something.'

'I... No, I don't want it. It would make me sick.' She looked around, eyes brimming. 'Who would do this, Marcus? And why? *Why?*'

He crouched in front of her, drawing her to him and holding her close as he smoothed his hand over her hair. 'I don't know, Eden. I wish I did!'

'All my things...' she said brokenly, leaning against him, drawing on his strength as she had never been able to do before and probably never would again.

'I know. But we'll sort it out.' He tipped her chin up and cupped her cheek, staring deep into her eyes, a strange expression in the depths of his. 'It will be all right, sweetheart. I promise.'

'Marcus, I——'

'Hello? Anyone home...?' Shiloh Smith stopped in the open doorway, his face suddenly grim as he looked around the room. When Marcus stood up and turned, he took a slow step inside. 'Looks like you've had visitors.'

'So it appears.' Marcus's tone fell far short of welcoming, his face set as he stared at the other man. 'Did you want something? Or is it just coincidence that you happened along this way?'

'Harry told me that the cottage was empty. When I saw lights on I stopped by just to check.' He turned to Eden, his gaze strangely intent. 'Have you any idea what they were after?'

She shook her head, standing unsteadily. 'None. There isn't—or rather wasn't—anything of value in the place apart from my paintings and they haven't taken them.' She looked around. 'It's such—such wanton, mindless destruction!'

'And we don't have the full picture yet.' Marcus claimed her attention, his tone unusually gentle as he continued, 'You need to check upstairs to see if anything is missing so we can tell the police.'

Eden glanced apprehensively towards the staircase. 'I suppose I'd better go up and take a look.'

'Do you want me to go?' Marcus offered quietly.

'No. I . . . I'll do it.' She walked slowly up the stairs, steeling herself, but the devastation was no better nor worse than what she'd seen down below. She picked up a few scattered items of lingerie tossed from one of the drawers then dropped them again, suddenly sickened by the thought of other, unseen hands touching them.

On shaking legs she started back downstairs and glanced round with a frown. 'Has he left already?'

Marcus dropped the crumpled sketch he'd been holding. 'Smith? Yes. There was no point in him staying.' He shot a speculative glance at the closed door. 'In fact I really wonder how he came to turn up here in the first place.'

Eden sighed, less interested in what Marcus was getting at than in the devastation which surrounded them. 'You heard what he said—that he saw lights and came to investigate.'

'Mmm, I heard all right but I can't help feeling it was just too convenient, the way he suddenly appeared. Exactly what do you know about him, Eden?'

Eden laughed hollowly. 'Not much...despite what you believe! Why? Just what are you getting at, Marcus? Surely you don't think that Shiloh Smith had a hand in this then came back to gloat?'

Marcus's mouth thinned. 'No. However, I have a feeling that his arrival here was more than mere coincidence.' He gave a sudden harsh laugh. 'Although I suppose the simple explanation could be that he was watching out for your return!'

Eden turned away without answering, refusing to be drawn into another pointless argument. She could tell Marcus until she was blue in the face that he was wrong about her and Smith but it wouldn't make a scrap of difference! And right at present she had enough to contend with.

She bent and picked up one of the drawers to try and fit it back into the dresser, stopping when Marcus came and took it from her and carefully set it back down on the floor.

'Leave it. You can't clear anything up until the police have been and checked this place for fingerprints.'

'Fingerprints?' Eden stared at him. 'Do you think they'll find any?'

'I've no idea but you're going to have to call them in if only to satisfy any insurance claims you need to make, and naturally they'll want to see if they can find any prints.' He looked round, his face suddenly determined. 'Frankly, I can't see any point in calling them tonight. Leave everything as it is and we can contact them in the morning.' He glanced at his watch. 'It's after midnight as it is and we need to find some place to stay.'

'Oh, but there's no need...'

'You can't stay here. That's obvious. No arguing, Eden. I really could do without that right now.'

She stiffened at the curt note in his voice. 'I'm sure you can. So could I! But there's no need to involve yourself in this, Marcus. It's my problem and I shall deal with it.'

'Correction, it's our problem!' He must have seen her start of surprise because he elaborated. 'If you hadn't gone away at my behest this weekend, this would never have happened, so I feel a certain responsibility to see that it is sorted out.'

He sounded so cold and aloof, his determination to help stemming merely from that highly developed sense of duty he possessed! Eden glared at him. 'Well, I relieve you of the responsibility! You don't need to worry about me. I'm well used to solving my own problems!'

He laughed softly, mockery glittering in the depths of his eyes. 'Is that a fact? You mean your numerous gentlemen friends don't lend a hand when it's needed? I wonder why I'm not surprised?'

She turned away, hurt by his sarcasm, and heard him sigh heavily.

'I apologise. That was uncalled for, in the circumstances. We have other, more pressing matters to deal with right now rather than going over old ground again.' When she started to protest he cut her off, steely determination in his eyes. 'No. I won't be swayed by anything you say. I suggest you pack whatever you need and then we'll find some place to stay the night. Unfortunately, the inn is booked solid, according to Smith, so we'll have to try the town.'

Eden looked away, wishing there were an alternative, but it was obvious that Marcus had every intention of seeing this through to the end his way. 'There's nothing I want, not after... after what's happened.'

Marcus said something rough under his breath as he immediately understood. He came and slid his hand under her elbow, his touch surprisingly gentle as he steered her towards the door and picked up her case. 'You should have enough in here to tide you over, but if you need anything we'll buy it. Now let's get out of here.'

He helped her into the car. Eden sighed as she leant her head back against the seat. It was going to take days to get the mess straightened out and then there was the problem of how much of her work had been ruined. Replacing it was going to be a problem just when the busy season was coming up. The area would be full of tourists over the next couple of months and they provided her with the income she needed to live on for the rest of the year. What a mess it all was... again!

'Are you all right?' There was genuine concern in Marcus's voice; it shocked her so much that she shot him a startled look. His hands tightened on the steering-wheel, his mouth drawing into a thin line. 'Don't look at me like that!'

'Like what?' she queried in confusion.

'As though I damn well terrify you!'

She gave a hollow laugh. 'I thought that was what you'd been aiming for since we met—terrifying me into submitting to your demands?'

He pulled the car over to the side of the road, letting the engine idle. 'That was never my intention.'

'No? Well, forgive me for jumping to entirely the wrong conclusion.' She gave a small forced laugh. 'Next time a man appears at my door issuing threats, I promise to give him the benefit of the doubt! Does that sound fair enough?'

'You could try the patience of a saint, do you know that?' he ground out, his eyes glittering fiercely. Eden felt a shiver run down her spine at his tone but one way and another she'd had enough for today, and it was a relief to find an outlet for her sudden anger.

'Is that how you see yourself, Marcus? As a saint?' she taunted.

'No, I damn well don't!' His eyes were like grey ice as they rested on her. 'I'm no saint, Eden, just a man like any other!'

'And I'm no sinner, Marcus. But sometimes, no matter how we try, people form the wrong impression of us, don't they?'

He laughed harshly. 'As I and so many others have formed the wrong impression of you? Oh, perhaps there are a few things about you I've not got to the bottom of yet but I'm not buying that!'

She couldn't stand it any longer, the insults, the contempt, this total refusal to see her in any light but the worst. She pushed the car door open, but before she could attempt to get out Marcus's hand closed around her wrist and hauled her back.

'Don't! I might just be tempted to leave you here. I'm sorry for what's happened to your home and I shall do all I can to help you get it sorted out, but it doesn't change my feelings towards you! Understand?' He stared at her for a long moment, letting her see that he meant what he said, then released her as he put the car into gear and pulled back on to the road.

Eden watched the countryside slipping past as they drove, wishing that there were some way to ease this agony she felt, but it would need Marcus's admission that he had been wrong about her to do that. And that was something which would never happen.

They booked in to a hotel in the nearby town, one of a large chain, where their arrival in the early hours of the morning passed without comment. Marcus completed all the formalities while Eden just stood aside and let him get on with it. She didn't really care what happened; she felt too tired and emotionally drained to cope with anything more.

When the porter showed them to connecting rooms on the third floor, she made no protest. She couldn't be safer from Marcus if she'd been locked away in a harem with an armed guard at the door! He wouldn't make advances towards a woman he loathed.

'Do you want anything to eat or drink? The receptionist told me that they run twenty-four-hour room service.' He paused in the doorway to the other room, big and cold and uncompromising as he watched her. Eden felt as though someone was slowly driving stakes through her heart but she hid her feelings. Letting Marcus see how easily he could hurt her was a mistake she had no intention of making.

'Nothing, thank you.' She turned to pick up her case and set it on the bed, opening it to draw out her toilet bag. She glanced back with a mocking lift of her brows when he continued to stand there watching her, making her heart ache even more. 'Is there something else you want, Marcus?'

His eyes narrowed, glittering slivers of ice as they skimmed her body in the close-fitting beige trousers and soft white sweater she'd worn to travel back. 'I don't think so.' His laughter was deliberately insulting. 'I think I'll pass on anything you might offer.'

Her cheeks flamed. 'It wasn't an offer! Don't flatter yourself! I'm not that desperate!'

'No?' He was across the room in two long strides, his face frankly scary as he backed her up against the bed. 'It didn't seem that way earlier on today. Surely you haven't forgotten that little interlude in the kitchen?' He grasped her chin and forced her eyes up to his. 'No, I can see you haven't. It was a pity we were so rudely interrupted, wasn't it? It can't be easy going without when you're used to a full sex life, and from what I've learned about you, my sweet, yours has been fuller than most.'

'And what was your excuse?' She laughed bitterly, hurting and wanting to hurt him back. 'Sure your memory isn't faulty, Marcus, if you don't recall that *you* were just as willing a participant in what went on?'

'Oh, there's nothing wrong with my memory. I have total recall of what happened from the moment you *accidentally* slipped by the lake to the way you were responding so eagerly and skilfully to my kisses.' He smiled thinly, running the pad of his thumb over her lower lip, sending a shooting flame of heat through her body. 'Such a talent for lovemaking must have taken a lot of practice.'

'It wasn't like that!' She tried to free herself but he wouldn't let her go as he bent closer and stared deep into her eyes in a way which made her suddenly realise what she was admitting.

'No?' The softness of the question scared her. It held a note which sent a frisson of fear racing through her body. What was she doing? If she told Marcus the truth—that she had wanted him desperately, that the desire she'd felt had owed nothing to experience but

everything to the fact that it had been *him* kissing her—
then the repercussions could be horrendous!

She took a steadying breath and forced a smile to lips
which felt numb. 'Well, not entirely.' Deliberately she
let her fingers trail up his chest. 'You are a very attractive man, Marcus. And a woman can't help
having...appetites.'

Contempt flashed across his face as he lifted her hands
away from him and pushed her away. 'But unfortunately I'm not on the menu, so, Eden, you will have to
go hungry a while longer.'

He turned and walked through to the connecting room,
closing the door quietly behind him. Eden picked up her
toilet bag and went into the bathroom, turning on the
shower before undressing and stepping under the needle-
sharp spray. And if there were tears mixed in with the
water running down her face then at least no one saw
them.

She was running, her breath coming in laboured spurts,
her muscles aching as she forced herself on. Up ahead
the figure stayed just out of reach no matter how hard
she tried to catch up with him. Broken china littered the
cliff-path under her feet, hampering her progress, and
she gasped out loud when one long shard pierced her
shoe, but she carried on running despite the pain.

She was closing the gap now, the man up ahead
slowing as he came to the edge of the cliffs. Eden carried
on running towards him, her feet flying over the sharp
pieces of china, and the torn scraps of paper. She was
almost there when he turned and held his arms out to
her. With a cry of joy Eden flung herself towards him
then heard the cry change to a scream of terror as he

suddenly disappeared and there was nothing between her and the jagged rocks below...

'Wake up! Eden, you're dreaming. Wake up!'

Hands shook her hard and she awoke with tears streaming down her face. For a moment she stared at Marcus, her eyes huge in a face the colour of parchment.

'You let me fall...on to the rocks!' She shuddered, the dream clinging to her mind, the horror of that moment when she had felt herself falling so real that a moan escaped her lips.

'It was a dream, Eden. Just a dream. You didn't fall.' He drew her to him, holding her close as he smoothed his hand down the tumbled length of her hair. 'I would never let anything like that happen to you.'

She gave a broken little sob. 'You hate me! You don't care if I live or die, Marcus.'

'No!' His tone was suddenly fierce, the hand smoothing her hair stilling as he drew her closer, a rigidity to his body which somehow shocked her.

She drew back to stare at him, watching the rapid play of emotions on his face without understanding any of them. He ran his thumbs across her wet cheeks, his touch achingly gentle.

'I don't want any harm to come to you, Eden.'

'Yet it would solve all your problems if I just simply disappeared off the face of the earth, wouldn't it?'

He went so still. Beneath her fingers she could feel the heavy beat of his heart, feel the steady rise and fall of his chest, yet he seemed to be carved from stone. 'That isn't what I want.'

'Maybe it isn't but sometimes I wish it would happen anyway!' She took a gulping breath, pain darkening her eyes. 'It hurts to know what you think of me, Marcus! It hurts to know you believe all those horrible lies!'

The dream and its aftermath had lowered her defences, making her admit things which only a short time before she had decided he must never know. Telling him this was madness because it made her so vulnerable yet the words just seemed to flow from her.

'Eden, I...' He groaned harshly, 'What the hell can I say? This all snowballed, turned into something I never anticipated! If I'd had any idea of what would happen then...'

'Then you would never have come to see me?' She laughed with bitter sadness. 'That's not true, Marcus. No matter what, you would still have come because it isn't in you to stand aside and see your sister get hurt if you can do anything about it. I envy her, you know. I don't think anyone has ever cared that much about me.'

'Your husband would have...if you'd played fair with him.' His voice was harsh and she winced but suddenly she was determined to set at least part of the record straight. She might not be able to tell him the truth about Eleanor and Rob Lewis, knew that he probably would never believe it, but it was up to her whether she broke her self-imposed silence about her marriage, and suddenly it seemed vitally important that Marcus should know!

'Geoff was incapable of that kind of unselfish love,' she said flatly. 'It wasn't in him to put anyone but himself first.'

Marcus gave a grim little laugh. 'That sounds very much like the pot calling the kettle!'

She met his gaze steadily. 'I imagine it does. Anyone who doesn't know the truth about what went on in our marriage would think that.'

'I think I know all the *truth* that I want to know!' He started to rise but Eden caught hold of his arm and held on, her eyes blazing at him.

'You haven't the first idea what the truth is! You've read those stories, listened to all those people, but the truth was never printed nor discussed! There are only two people who know what happened—myself and Geoff—and Geoff is dead and I'm to be forever damned for keeping quiet and not wanting his family to get hurt more than they have been!'

'If you imagine that I'm interested in this then you're wrong!' He tried to prise her fingers from his arm but Eden held on with a strength which surprised them both.

'Of course you should be interested, Marcus! You told me yourself that you always make a point of finding out all you can about an adversary, and that's what I am, isn't that right? So can you afford not to listen and learn?'

'This is ridiculous. It's late and you're overwrought,' he grated out.

'Perhaps I am, and perhaps telling you this will do me the world of good.' Eden tossed the long strands of hair back from her flushed face, feeling her heart beating rapidly with a wild kind of desperation. 'Geoff was insanely jealous. Every time I looked at another man, and I do mean *looked*, he started a row about it. It got to the point where I dreaded going out in case we met anyone and I would be accused of anything from trying to pick him up to wanting to sleep with him!'

'I don't want to hear any more!' Marcus stood up, breaking her hold on his arm as he towered over her, his face glacial.

'I'm sure you don't. It doesn't make pleasant listening. It was even worse to try and live with!' She laughed harshly, feeling hysteria bubbling to the surface. 'Can you imagine having to watch every word you say, weigh up every smile, all the time wondering if you've done anything which could possibly be construed as provocative? It got to the point where I almost started to believe the accusations myself! That's how low my self-esteem had got. But in my heart I always *knew* that I had done none of the things Geoff accused me of.' She stared up at him, her eyes meeting his and holding them. 'I never had an affair while I was married. There were no other men at all! It was all in Geoff's mind. His jealousy was a sort of illness; it wasn't rational or logical, it had no basis in fact but was the result of his own tortured mind. Do you believe me, Marcus?'

She held her breath, waiting to hear his answer, knowing that it was desperately important to her that he should try to believe what she had told him. If he took that one step then surely it would make it easier for him to take the next and accept that he had been wrong about her and Rob? Once she had cleared it with Eleanor and made her see how important it was, then she was going to tell him!

'Marcus, I——'

He cut her off, his face never softening as he stared down at her. 'Maybe you can claim not to have had an affair while you were married and maybe it's true, but one thing I know for a fact is that you had one with Becky's husband. So explain that away if you can, Eden!'

He turned and left the room without a backward glance. Eden lay back against the pillows, closing her eyes on a huge wave of defeat. It had made no difference what she had told him; it hadn't softened his attitude towards her, nor made her try to see that he could be wrong. Marcus would never feel anything but contempt for her and to try to change that would merely be to inflict more pain upon herself. Far better that she accept it and try to put him out of her life rather than keep on hoping for what could never be.

She lay sleeplessly until dawn broke then got up and dressed and packed. If the receptionist on duty thought it at all odd that she should leave at such an hour, she said nothing as she made up the bill for the night's stay. When Eden handed her the note she'd written for Marcus, curtly informing him that she didn't require his help to sort out the damage at the cottage, the girl took it with just the faintest flicker of curiosity, which she quickly disguised.

Eden left the hotel, a bitter smile on her mouth as the irony struck her. The receptionist most probably thought that she and Marcus had had some kind of lovers' quarrel and that was why she was sneaking away. If only she knew the truth! She and Marcus might have pretended to be lovers this weekend but that was something they would never truly be!

CHAPTER NINE

IT TOOK two full days to clear up after the police had finished but although they'd dusted for fingerprints they'd found none. As the inspector in charge of investigations had rather curtly informed Eden, it had been a professional job. The fact that there was nothing missing had seemed to arouse his interest. He'd asked a lot of searching questions but Eden had been unable to give any reason as to why anyone should want to cause so much damage to her home.

It was all very odd and left her feeling vaguely uneasy. Was there something going on which she was unaware of? She pondered on it as she walked to the village with Drac bounding along at her side. It was a glorious morning, a warm breeze sending whitecaps skittering across the bay. Shiloh Smith's yacht was still lying at anchor but she'd seen nothing of him since the night of the break-in. That too seemed strange because she'd half expected him to call again.

She mentioned his disappearance to Harry when she called at the inn to leave another of her paintings which had mercifully escaped the damage that so many others had suffered.

'No, I've not seen him for a couple of days, Miss Moore.' Harry picked up a glass. 'Seems he's another who's disappeared.'

'Another?' Eden frowned.

'Aye. It was the strangest thing. I let two rooms out to a couple of foreigners—Italians, I think they were.

They paid in advance yet the following morning when the missus went to make the beds they'd never been slept in and we've not seen hide nor hair of them since.'

'How strange. Do you remember which night it was, Harry?'

Harry breathed on the glass then gave it another turn of the cloth. 'I do that. Same night as your place was broken into.'

'How odd.'

Harry shrugged. 'Probably just a coincidence, I expect.'

Eden nodded, unwilling to admit to anyone else the unease she felt in case she was finding mysteries where they didn't exist! She bit back a sigh as she said goodbye and set off for the post office to buy some stamps. Life had been so simple before Marcus had upset it and now at every turn the strangest things kept happening!

Her heart gave a familiar little lurch at the thought of him. She had tried her hardest to put him out of her mind and keep him out but it had proved impossible. He'd made no attempt to contact her, obviously preferring to leave things as they were. If only it were that easy to put an end to it. Marcus had come into her life uninvited, unwelcome, yet his leaving had left behind a huge void. If it hadn't sounded completely crazy she would have said that she *missed* him! But why on earth should she miss someone who held her in such contempt?

She sighed as she opened the door to the post office. Somewhere at the very back of her mind lay the answer to that question but she wasn't going to dig too deep and find it. Something told her that discovering the truth would only bring more heartache, and that was something she could do without!

'Oh, I'm glad you stopped by, Miss Moore. There's a letter for you. Perhaps it's the one you've been waiting for?'

Eden took it from the woman behind the counter, experiencing a relief which was short-lived when she realised the handwriting wasn't Eleanor's. She purchased her stamps then went outside and sat on that harbour wall, ripping the envelope open and glancing first at the signature. Shock and a strange, icy apprehension filled her as she read it. What on earth was Eleanor's fiancé, Ben, writing to her about?

The letter was brief, its tone hinting at the anger Ben had been feeling when he had written it. He was writing, he said, to inform her that he and Eleanor were no longer together and enclosing an address where she could be contacted. As far as he was concerned that was the end of the matter!

Eden bit back a shocked little gasp. She could only assume that Ben had found out about Eleanor's affair with Rob Lewis. He had every right to be angry and hurt, of course, but why had it all come out now? Unless... Her stomach gave a sickening little lurch. *Unless* the affair wasn't over but still going on!

She shot to her feet, stumbling as she started to run back to the cottage. Drac bounded along, barking happily, enjoying the game, but this wasn't a game! If Eleanor was still seeing Rob and Marcus found out then there was no knowing what might happen! She had to see Eleanor at once and make her understand exactly what was at stake!

The journey seemed to take forever. Eden sat on the edge of the train seat all the way, unaware of the hustle and bustle going on around her. When the taxi dropped her off in front of the expensive mews house, she took a deep breath and told herself to stay calm. She might have been wrong, might have jumped to all sorts of hasty conclusions!

She closed her eyes and felt a shudder run through her as a face sprang instantly to mind, the face which haunted her dreams and every unguarded moment. If she wasn't wrong then God help them when Marcus found out!

Squaring her shoulders, she rang the bell, hearing quick footsteps coming along the hall before the door was flung open.

'You're early...Eden! What on earth are you doing here?'

There was less welcome than shock in Eleanor's voice. Eden felt a sudden chill but forced herself to smile. 'Hello, Eleanor. I've been trying to get hold of you for some time but obviously you've moved.'

Eleanor glanced along the street with a trace of nervousness. 'Yes, obviously.'

'So you didn't receive my letter?'

'I...' Eleanor shrugged a shade defiantly. 'Of course I got it. I've just been too busy to write back. I'm rather busy at the moment, in fact.'

'Then the sooner we get this sorted out the better.' Eden stared pointedly at the door and after a momentary hesitation Eleanor held it open then led the way into a small sitting-room at the rear of the house. She walked to a table by the window, took a cigarette out of a box and lit it, her hands shaking as she put the lighter down again and glanced back at Eden.

'I suppose I can guess why you're here—to do your big sister act and tell me off for being a naughty girl, I imagine.'

'What do you expect me to say, Eleanor? That it was all right to use my name and involve me in this mess?'

Eleanor had the grace to flush. She looked away, taking a long draw on the cigarette before asking abruptly, 'How did you find out I was here?'

'From Ben.'

'Ben? You've spoken to him? How is he? What did he say?' Eleanor's face suddenly paled. She crushed the cigarette out in an ashtray then sank down on to a chair as all her previous bravado disappeared. 'Did . . . did he ask about me?'

Eden sat down opposite and shook her head. 'No. I didn't speak to him. He wrote a letter telling me where you were living now and that you and he were through.'

Sudden tears welled in Eleanor's eyes and she lowered her head. 'I see.'

'What on earth has been going on, Eleanor?' Eden leant forward, catching her sister's trembling hands between both of hers. 'I wrote asking that very same question and you claim you were too busy to reply yet I think I'm entitled to an answer, don't you?' She gave a sudden bitter laugh and sat back in the chair. 'Seeing as you made free with my name and got me involved in this, that's the least I'm due!'

'I never meant this to happen! You have to believe me, Eden!' There was a sudden urgency in Eleanor's voice.

'Then why use my name in the first place?' It was impossible to hide her anger and Eleanor got up and walked to the window.

'I should have thought that was obvious,' she said hollowly. 'I used your name so that I wouldn't be found out but it didn't work out as I hoped it would.'

She swung round, her eyes holding a pleading light. 'I would never have done it if I'd realised that you'd be drawn into it! There didn't seem any harm in it at first. It was only later that everything started to go wrong!'

'When Marcus Cole discovered that you'd been having an affair with his brother-in-law, you mean?'

Eleanor turned away, but not before Eden had seen the guilt on her face. 'Yes.'

'But why did you do it? I thought that you and Ben were happy. Oh, I know there'd been a few rough patches but you seemed to be getting over them.'

'We were but then the same things started to go wrong all over again.' Eleanor paced the room, too restless and on edge to keep still. 'It isn't much of an excuse but I honestly didn't intend to get...involved with Rob. It was just that Ben was always busy working. He was never home, night after night, but I suppose the final straw was when he went away on a business trip to the States. I was at a very low point then, missing him yet furious with him for leaving me alone and then...then I met Rob at a cocktail party one night.'

She closed her eyes with a weary sigh, as though this was something she had gone over many times before in her mind. 'It was just a fling, I thought, a bit of excitement which could do no harm so long as no one found out. That's when I came up with the idea of using your name as a safeguard.'

'I see. So Rob didn't know who you really were?'

'Not at first. We only saw one another a couple of times, including that weekend in Edinburgh. Then Ben came back and I suddenly realised what I had done, what it would do to our relationship if he found out. I told Rob that I didn't want to see him again and thought— hoped!—that was the end of it. Ben and I went away on holiday and everything seemed to be marvellous, just like it used to be. But then we got back home and...'

'And what?' Eden prompted as her sister hesitated.

'And I found your letter waiting and Rob came to see me. I had no idea what he was talking about. He kept going on about how I should act at the wedding, how careful I must be when I spoke to his wife...!' Eleanor's look was pleading as she stopped her pacing. 'I didn't know he was married, Eden! You must believe that.'

Eden nodded, feeling relieved. Eleanor had been wrong to do what she had but at least she hadn't wilfully set about ruining Becky's marriage. 'I do believe you. And I'm so pleased to hear it. But what you're saying is that Rob only found out who you really were when he came to see you before the wedding? And, consequently, who I was?'

'Yes. I didn't know what to do! Rob seemed to think it was terribly funny that this Marcus Cole had been misled as well. Oh, I wanted to tell everyone the truth but I was scared, afraid that Ben would find out and what it could mean! And Rob said that it would be better to say nothing as once the weekend was over that would be the end of it. I felt so guilty at what I'd let you in for but it seemed to make a certain kind of sense.... If I left well alone then that would be the end of it.'

'Only it wasn't, was it?' Eden asked quietly. 'How did Ben find out?'

Tears welled in Eleanor's eyes again and trickled down her face. 'I don't know! I didn't tell him. I couldn't believe it when I got home one day and he challenged me about it!' She took a deep breath, struggling for composure, but it was obvious that she found talking about what had happened between her and Ben painful. 'I— I tried to deny it at first, but he wouldn't listen, just

went on and on about how he *knew*, until in the end I
screamed at him that it was true, that I'd had an affair
and that it was all his fault because he was always so
wrapped up in his work, he never spared any time for
me.'

'Oh, Eleanor! You know that isn't true. Ben loves you!
He always has. If he was working hard then it was for
both of you.'

'I know, I know! I can see that now but it was all
getting on top of me and I wasn't thinking clearly.' She
drew a tissue from her skirt pocket and wiped her eyes
then gave a bitter laugh. 'I must be jinxed. I hurt
everyone I love, don't I? First Mum and Dad and then
you and...and Ben!'

'You mustn't think that way!' Eden got up and gave
her sister a hug. 'It's rubbish, utter rubbish!'

'Is it?' Eleanor's face was pleading. 'Then you don't
hate me for this, Eden, all the trouble I've caused by
making you go to that wedding and pretend to be me?'

Eleanor didn't know the half of it! She had no idea
of the problems she had caused but it would serve no
purpose in telling her. Eden walked over to the window
and stared out with hollow eyes at the tiny garden where
a few roses were beginning to bloom. 'No, of course I
don't hate you.' She glanced round, looking straight at
Eleanor so there could be no misunderstanding. 'But you
must promise that this is the end of it and that you won't
see Rob ever again.'

Eleanor looked suddenly uncomfortable. She twisted
the tissue between her hands, avoiding Eden's eyes. 'I
don't know if I can do that,' she whispered.

'What?' Eden swung round, aghast. 'For heaven's
sake, Eleanor, he's a married man! Surely that's reason
enough to stay away from him, quite apart from the re-

percussions it could have for all of us?' Her hands clenched at her sides as she fought for control, knowing that she had to make Eleanor understand the urgency of the situation. 'Marcus Cole threatened to go to the papers and rake up all that old business about Geoff if I...or rather *you* kept on seeing Rob!'

'What?' Eleanor's face was blank with shock. 'But it was all lies, every bit of it. The papers exaggerated everything Geoff's relatives said!'

'I know that and you know that but Cole believes every word that was written, it seems.' Suddenly all the energy drained out of her and Eden leant against the wall as she ran a weary hand across her face. 'That's why it's imperative that you stay well away from Rob in future. I...I don't think I could go through all that again.'

'I had no idea...' Eleanor took a shaky breath, her face waxen. 'You don't deserve this, Eden. It isn't fair!'

Eden gave a wry smile. 'Who said life is supposed to be fair? But just promise that you'll do as I ask and that should be the end of it.'

'You don't understand, Eden. I...I can't promise you that.' Eleanor's tone was pleading; it sent a chill of apprehension flowing through Eden's whole body. She stared at Eleanor, her whole body trembling with a sudden fear.

'Why? Why can't you make that promise? Tell me!'

'It's quite simple... Because Eleanor and I are leaving the country together tomorrow.'

Eden spun round, her eyes widening when she saw - Rob Lewis in the doorway. She hadn't heard him come in and now she went cold when she saw the expression on his face as he smiled at her.

'I see that comes as a shock but I'm sure that you'll be glad that your sister has found happiness again? After all, the reason you didn't tell dear Marcus the truth right at the beginning was because you wanted Eleanor to be happy, and she will be... with me.'

He came further into the room, sliding his arm across Eleanor's shoulders as he stared at Eden with a smile which sent a wave of sickness to the pit of her stomach. 'You and Marcus seem to have a common bond in that respect. What a pity that he's going to take your part in this so badly.'

Eden licked her parched lips, looking from him to Eleanor, but her sister was staring down at the floor. She looked back at Rob and shook her head. 'No,' she said, then repeated it with more force. 'No!'

He raised his brows. 'You don't agree? You think that Marcus will overlook the way you've tricked him?' He gave a sudden harsh laugh which made her flinch. 'Perhaps you and my dear brother-in-law are closer than I realised even after witnessing that touching little scene in the kitchen!'

Eden's face flamed with embarrassment, bile rising into her throat at the tone in Rob's voice which turned something magical into something sordid. 'I didn't trick Marcus! You did. You knew before the wedding that Eleanor had been using my name! All you needed to do was tell him that when we met!'

'Mmm, I suppose I could have done but you seemed to be intent on carrying through the masquerade so who was I to spoil things? Oh, what tangled webs we weave... no matter how noble the intentions. But unfortunately that doesn't alter the fact that Marcus will be furious when he finds out the truth, although by then it will be far too late for him to do anything about it.' ·

'You think so? You really imagine that he will let you get away with this?' Eden turned to her sister, her voice echoing with emotion. 'You can't do this, Eleanor. You know it's wrong! What about Ben?'

Eleanor's face was ashen, her eyes full of pain as she raised her head at last. 'Ben doesn't care about me. He told me he never wants to see me again. I...I'm not like you, Eden. I'm not strong enough to cope by myself. Rob...Rob and I are going to start a new life together and put the past behind us.'

'And how do you put behind you the fact that he's married? Can you live with that, Eleanor? Can you start a new life on that basis?'

Eleanor looked away, biting her lip to hold back fresh tears. 'Rob's marriage was over before we ever met. He told me that and I...I believe him!'

It probably was. It was probably the one true thing that Lewis had ever said. No marriage could survive if one partner was intent on destroying it. Undoubtedly Becky would be better off without Lewis, but no one had the right to decide that for her. She would be devastated when she found out, and Marcus...Marcus would be furious with everyone concerned—especially her, because she had, unwittingly, played along with the deception and in his eyes encouraged this to happen!

Suddenly, Eden couldn't take any more; the thought of Marcus's rage was more than she could stand. She turned and ran from the room, ignoring Eleanor's imploring cry to stop as she ran out into the street. She ran halfway down the road then stopped and leant against the wall as she tried to collect herself and think what to do but her head was spinning from all she had found out. The one cold, clear thought she had was that Marcus would hate her more than ever now!

'You never damn well learn, do you? Did you really imagine that you could get away with it? Well, this time, Eden, you've gone too far!'

The shock of hearing Marcus's voice on top of everything else was so great that she swayed and would have fallen if she hadn't clutched hold of the wall. 'Marcus, I...'

He caught her by the wrist, his long fingers bruising as they tightened until she whimpered in pain. 'You lying, deceitful little slut! You stayed in Becky's house, pretended to accept the friendship she offered you, yet you still can't keep your hands off her husband!' He hauled her to him, glaring down into her white face, a wildness in his eyes which scared her. 'So help me, Eden, you'll pay for this!'

'No! Marcus, you must listen. It isn't what you think!' She tried to free herself but he still held her, staring at her in a way which made her heart break. He would find out the truth, of course. But in the end it would make no difference. Marcus would always hate her and she couldn't bear it because... because she loved him!

The sudden realisation shocked her so that she cried out but Marcus misinterpreted the reason for her distress, his eyes narrowing cruelly. 'Isn't it? I don't know the full story, is that what you're saying? Then why don't we go back and have a word with Lewis and find out exactly what has been going on? What a good job I decided to follow him today, although I must confess that I never expected to find you here.'

He hauled her back to the house, his face set and uncompromising, his grey eyes like ice as they rested on her shocked face. He smiled unpleasantly. 'What's the matter, sweetheart? Afraid that Lewis will blame it all on you again?' He laughed dangerously, bending to stare directly into her eyes. 'And maybe it's the truth. Did you seek him out again, Eden, because you couldn't bear the thought of him having found someone else to replace you? What did you use to arouse his interest again—that delectable body of yours?'

His eyes slid over her in a look which sent a shaft of ice-cold fear slicing through her. 'God knows you're temptation enough to make it difficult for any man to resist you!'

He knocked on the door, that cruel, taunting smile still shaping his mouth. Eden struggled wildly, wanting only to get free and run from the whole nightmare, but suddenly the door opened and it was too late, for she saw Rob Lewis standing there. For a moment shock seemed to rob him of the ability to speak as he stared at her and Marcus before Marcus broke the silence.

'Surprised to see us?' Marcus's voice held a note which made Lewis pale, the smile he gave him little short of predatory. When the man made no attempt to reply, he laughed aloud. 'I never thought I'd see the day when you'd be lost for a glib word or two! Still, it just goes to show, doesn't it?'

Rob made an obvious effort to regain his composure, but his face was strained, his eyes full of a fear that Eden could understand. She could feel the tension in Marcus, knew without a shadow of a doubt that he was waiting only for an excuse before the violence she could sense in him erupted. And a sudden fear of what might happen unloosed her tongue.

'Marcus, this won't achieve anything! Can't you see that?'

'Frankly, no.' He barely spared her a glance as he pushed her inside the house. He closed the door and leant back against it, his eyes cutting straight to Rob

Lewis's shocked face. 'I warned you what to expect, didn't I? What a pity you didn't heed that warning...both of you. I had the feeling that there was something going on, which is why I followed you here today, Rob, and it seems I was right.'

Eden stared from one to the other, her heart thundering as the tension grew. Then, just as she thought she couldn't stand it a second longer, there was the sound of footsteps and Eleanor's light tones carried along the hall.

'Who is it, Rob? Has Eden come back? Make her come in while we talk about this.'

The expression on Marcus's face would have been comical if Eden had felt at all like laughing. Shock tightened every muscle, turned his grey eyes silvery as they centred on the woman who suddenly appeared. For a long moment no one spoke, the silence humming until it hurt their ears. Then Rob Lewis laughed, the sound echoing round and round, ugly and bitter, tainting the air with its savage enjoyment of the situation.

'Allow me to make the introductions, Marcus. I don't believe that you've met Eden's sister, have you?' He looked from Eleanor's shocked face to Eden's strained one and laughed again. 'The resemblance is quite remarkable, isn't it? It's no wonder you were fooled! It seems the joke's on you, brother-in-law, after all.'

There was a moment, just one, when Eden stood and stared at the silent little tableau: Rob smiling as he enjoyed his moment of triumph, Eleanor gradually losing that frozen look of shock, and Marcus...Marcus staring at *her* with a dawning comprehension and contempt which cut her to the quick!

Then, with a cry of distress, she pushed past him and ran, not stopping when behind her she heard the angry roar of his voice shouting her name. She couldn't stop... *wouldn't* go back and see his eyes filled with that contempt and hatred! She loved him, but now more than ever that seemed like the biggest mistake she had ever made!

CHAPTER TEN

NIGHT had fallen by the time Eden started down the path to the cottage. She stumbled as her foot caught on a loose rock and felt a sharp stab of pain at the memory of that first night and how Marcus had fallen in almost the same way. So much had happened since then that it seemed as though it had happened in another lifetime when she'd been a different person from the woman she was now, loving a man who hated her!

Tears stung her eyes but she couldn't cry. There could be no release from this agony because it wasn't over yet. Marcus would never let it end like this; he would want to exact some kind of retribution for what she had done!

She reached the bottom of the path and took her key from her bag then stopped uncertainly when she saw that the cottage door was open. For a moment she stood and stared at it, feeling her heart give a sickening little lurch of alarm as she suddenly realised how quiet it was. Usually Drac would be going frantic by now, barking a greeting as he heard her footsteps. Now the silence and a deep sense of something being wrong filled her with fear.

On leaden legs she took the last couple of steps and pushed the door open the final inch needed to look inside but all appeared much as she'd left it. Hesitantly, she went in, leaving the door open as she felt her way to the table and struck a match to light the lamp.

'Drac! Where are you boy?' she called, and was re-warded by a faint whine from the direction of the kitchen. Picking up the lamp, she started across the room, then felt the blood drain from her head when an unfamiliar voice said softly, 'I think it would be better if you left the animal where he is, Miss Moore.'

Eden whirled round, holding the lamp aloft as she stared towards the shadows by the stairs. 'Who's there? What do you want?'

A figure came forward then stopped just beyond the circle of light cast by the lamp. 'Who I am is not important. As for what I want...' The man shrugged. 'It started out as a simple request for information. Unfortunately, that has changed.'

Eden frowned, trying to hold at bay the icy fear which was stealing through her body. 'I have no idea what you're talking about. Look, if this is some kind of joke...!'

The man laughed, not a pleasant sound—it sent a shiver rippling down her spine, intensified her fear, and she took a quick step backwards then suddenly became aware that there was someone behind her, another man standing in the doorway. She spun round, thrusting the lamp in front of her, but the face she saw was that of a stranger.

'Ah, you English with your love of jokes! You always imagine that others share your strange sense of humour. But unfortunately, Miss Moore, this is no joke!'

Eden swung back, staring through the shadows, only then becoming aware that the man, although speaking perfect English, had an accent. What was it—French, Spanish...Italian? She couldn't explain yet for some reason she knew there was a clue there if she could only work it out, but her brain seemed to have frozen as the fear seeped into every pore.

When she said nothing the man gave another one of those unpleasant laughs. 'It is rare to find a woman who asks so few questions. Perhaps that is the reason why your boyfriend values you so highly?'

'Boyfriend?' She forced down her mounting panic. She had to stay calm, buy herself some time—but time for what? No one would call—no one ever had at this time of the night...apart from Marcus! She stared at the man with huge shocked eyes. 'Has this anything to do with...with Marcus?'

'Signor Cole? No. But how interesting that his name should spring to mind first. Perhaps your relationship with Signor Lewis isn't what he led us to believe? Still, no matter, eh? It will serve our purpose.'

Lewis? Rob Lewis? What had this to do with him? What was going on? Eden had no idea yet she could feel herself starting to shake at the note in the man's voice. 'What do you want?' she demanded hoarsely.

'What we want is to teach your friend Signor Lewis a lesson. Unfortunately he hasn't been co-operating as we would wish. He needs to be shown that we are not playing games, nor, indeed, making jokes.' The man shrugged again. 'It is unfortunate that you, Miss Moore, will be instrumental in teaching him that.'

He nodded to the other man who moved so fast that Eden had no time to avoid him as he caught hold of her. Taking the lamp from her, he set it down on the table. Eden struggled wildly, fear and panic overwhelming her. 'What are you doing? Let me go!'

Her voice rose and beyond the closed kitchen door she heard Drac barking frantically but the man ignored the frenzied sound, speaking curtly to his accomplice who dragged Eden outside and across the grass to where the white fence formed a fragile barrier against the edge of the cliff.

Eden gave a shocked little scream, her struggles intensifying as she suddenly realised what they intended. 'No! Don't! No!'

Her cries cut through the night, closely followed by the sound of shattering glass. Eden looked back to see Drac racing around the house towards them, snarling ferociously. The man holding her uttered a startled cry, his grip slackening for a moment, and Eden took immediate advantage of the opportunity. With a sharp twist of her body she broke free and ran, avoiding the other man who tried to step in her way as she raced towards the path which led down to the cove. Behind her she could hear angry shouting and Drac's snarling but she didn't dare stop to look back as her feet flew over the rough ground.

Reaching the bottom, she chanced a glance over her shoulder and felt her heart stop when she saw a figure coming after her. With a cry of fear, she set off across the rocks, expecting at any moment to feel hard hands catch her...

'Eden!'

It was Marcus's voice shouting her name! Despite the roaring of the surf as it broke against the rocks, the thundering of her own terrified heartbeat, she would know those deep tones anywhere!

Shock and total disbelief made her look back just as a huge wave washed over the rocks, dragging her feet from under her. She pitched sideways into the water, catching the side of her head on the rocks as she fell. There was a roaring in her ears, a burning in her lungs, then darkness which seemed to go on and on...

Her body heaved, forcing out the sea water. Eden dragged in air, her lungs aching.

'That's it. You've done it. Thank God!'

It was Shiloh Smith's voice. Eden recognised it even through the haze in her mind and she frowned as she tried to work out what was going on. However, before she could manage it she felt herself being lifted from the cold ground as strong arms closed around her and in some inexplicable way she knew that it was Marcus who was holding her.

'Marcus...what...what's happening?' Her voice was faint and raspy; it shocked her to hear the hoarse sound of it, so that her eyes flew open and met his. He stared down at her, grey eyes burning with an emotion which made her feel almost as breathless as she'd done moments before.

'Don't try to talk. I'm taking you back to the cottage. You're safe now.' His arms tightened around her, holding her close as though *he* needed the reassurance as much as she! It shocked her into silence until she saw the group of people gathered in front of the cottage. One of the group stepped forward and opened the door so that Marcus could carry her inside, speaking to him in a low undertone, and with a start Eden recognised Flynn O'Rourke!

'Marcus, what's going on?' she demanded shakily. 'Who are these people? And why is Flynn here?' She looked round. 'Drac! Where is he? Is he all right?'

He shifted her so that her body was pressed against the hard wall of his chest as he kicked the door shut behind him. 'He's fine despite the fact that he jumped through the kitchen window when he heard you screaming. One of O'Rourke's men has taken him into town to the vet's just to make certain but apart from a few cuts he seems to be perfectly all right. As to the rest, well, I'll explain it all later. For now let's just get you sorted out. You really need to see a doctor.'

She shook her head, biting back a moan at the resultant throbbing. 'I don't want a doctor! What I need is to find out what's going on!'

His lips curled into a smile which did alarming things to her heartbeat. 'You really are enough to try the patience of a——'

'Saint!' She glared at him. 'But we've already established that you aren't one of those!'

He stared deeply into her angry eyes. 'Not with you around, Eden, I'm not!'

His tone laid a disturbing new emphasis on the statement which knocked her sideways and she was still reeling when he set her gently down on a chair in front of the fireplace. He turned to go but Eden caught his arm as fear rose swiftly, carried along by the sudden resurgence of memory. 'Don't go, Marcus! Please don't leave me.'

He stopped at once, his face set in the soft glow from one of the lamps which someone must have lit. 'I'm not going anywhere. I just want to make the fire.'

'Oh.' There didn't seem anything else she could say right then. She leant back and closed her eyes, trying to blank out how afraid she'd been when those two men had dragged her towards the edge of the cliffs...

A sob escaped her lips before she could stop it and she heard Marcus say something harsh as he dropped the armful of logs on to the floor in front of the grate then crouched down beside the chair. 'Don't! It's over now, I promise you!'

Her violet eyes were dark with memories as they lifted to his. 'I was so scared, Marcus,' she whispered brokenly. 'I think they meant to... to kill me!'

He cupped her cheek, his hand trembling. 'I was scared too. When you fell into the sea I thought that was it, that I wouldn't be able to get to you!'

The horror of that moment shone in his eyes before he straightened abruptly. He turned away to start the fire, fanning the flames until they began to blaze brightly, making Eden suddenly conscious of just how cold she was. Shivers danced up and down her body and she wrapped her arms tightly around herself but it seemed impossible to warm the chill from her icy flesh.

'You must get out of those wet clothes.' Marcus's voice was level, almost impersonal now. Eden nodded, trying hard to match his mood, but when she tried to stand to go upstairs to undress she found she didn't have the strength.

She sank back on to the chair, tears spilling from her eyes, and heard Marcus curse softly although somehow she knew it wasn't her display of weakness which angered him.

He turned and ran upstairs, reappearing just minutes later with a quilt he had taken from her bed and a towel from the bathroom. He dropped them onto the floor in front of the fire then lifted Eden gently to her feet. Her clothes were soaked with sea water, clinging to her, but Marcus peeled the sodden garments from her one by one and tossed them aside until she stood there naked in the firelight.

She shivered as the warmth assailed her icy skin yet even reaching for the quilt seemed too much of an effort. Perhaps she should feel embarrassed at standing there and allowing Marcus to help her like this but it didn't seem wrong, not when his hands moved so deftly and gently as he picked up the towel and started to rub her dry.

Once he was certain that her skin was free of any moisture, he picked up the quilt and cocooned her in its folds, his face devoid of all emotion so that she knew she must have imagined feeling his hands trembling as he drew it around her.

There was a sudden knock at the door and Marcus eased her back down into the chair before going to answer it. He spoke quietly to whoever was outside then came back across the room to stop beside the fire and stare into the glowing flames.

'That was Flynn. I told him that you didn't want to see a doctor.'

Eden pushed the wet length of her hair away from her face. 'I don't. I'll be fine in a while.'

Marcus shot her a quick, assessing glance. 'You had a nasty knock on your head quite apart from the scare you must have had; you should see someone just to be on the safe side.'

'Perhaps I will...later. Not just yet. I...I don't want to go anywhere just yet. I just want to stay here!'

Her voice broke and she turned away, hiding her distress as best she could.

'Don't, Eden. I've told you, it's over. There's no need to be afraid any more.'

There was a hollow note of regret and pain in his deep voice which brought her eyes to his face while she studied the hard planes and angles which the flickering firelight only seemed to emphasise. She loved him so much! How or why it should have happened was an unanswerable question. He had given her no reason to fall in love with him, would probably refuse to believe her even if she tried to tell him, but it didn't alter how she felt. And accepting it was both a joy and a deep sadness.

She looked away from him, fighting for control. All that was left to her now was dignity, the strength to handle this without breaking down and allowing Marcus to know that her heart was breaking. 'What was going on tonight, Marcus? Who were those men and what did they want?'

His hands clenched into fists, every bone in his face standing out sharply in relief. 'You got involved in something you shouldn't have, Eden!'

'You mean the affair between my sister and...and Rob Lewis?' she asked haltingly.

His eyes blazed at her, steel-hard, glittering with an anger which cut her. 'Yes! Do you have any idea what kind of danger you were in tonight...do you?' He bent to glare at her, catching her chin to force her to meet his eyes.

She shuddered, not proof against that anger when all her senses were raw. 'Yes,' she whispered. 'But I still don't understand. I don't understand who those men were or what they wanted!'

Marcus let her go abruptly, turning back to stare into the flames again. 'What they wanted was to scare Rob Lewis into giving them some information. They were prepared to go to any lengths to get it.'

'One of them said something of the sort—but what information? And why should it be so valuable?' She sat forward, unaware that the quilt slipped from one shoulder and that in the flickering glow of the fire her skin gleamed as smooth and pale as alabaster.

Marcus's gaze lingered on her for a long moment before his face tautened and he looked away. 'It all centres on a fraud case which went to court recently in

Rome. The key witness to the case, a man called Alessi, fled to England before the trial, fearing for his life. When there was an extradition order granted by the government, forcing him to return, he came to me to see if I could do anything to stop it being put into force. I finally persuaded him that he should go back and testify before the court, but arranged that he would have protection.

'There were only two people who knew where Alessi was being held before the trial—myself and Flynn O'Rourke, who was in charge of the security operation. Yet an attempt was made on Alessi's life. Obviously there had been some kind of leak; O'Rourke knew it wasn't from his end so I became the number one suspect.'

'But that's ridiculous. Anyone who knows you would realise you couldn't be involved!'

She flushed as his brows raised at her vehement denial and looked away as he continued in the same, flat tone. 'There was a vast amount of money at stake, enough to tempt anyone. However, you're right—it hadn't come from me and O'Rourke eventually was satisfied about that, but his investigations pointed to the fact that it had come from my end!' His mouth thinned, tension coiling his body tightly at the thought.

'And Rob Lewis was responsible?' Eden guessed. 'But how?'

'How did he gain access to something so potentially harmful? Sheer chance. He overheard a phone call between myself and O'Rourke then stumbled across a file in the office listing O'Rourke's name in relation to another case where a witness had needed protection.' Marcus sighed heavily. 'I think he merely put two and two together and hit the jackpot. He had contacts in the underworld so it didn't take long for him to strike a deal and sell what he knew. But it didn't end there. Alessi went to court and testified and his evidence sent several very important men to gaol for a long time. However, they have all appealed against their sentences and Alessi's testimony will be crucial once again to the outcome of those appeals...if he's around to give it.'

'So he's still in danger? How awful!' Eden couldn't hide her shock.

Marcus smiled grimly. 'There's a lot at stake, vast sums of money, and, frankly, those involved will stop at nothing. Alessi has been given a new identity and a new life in another country but that hasn't deterred them. They wanted Lewis to find out where Alessi is. I think he's been playing them along, getting more cash off them, but they must have lost patience with him. Tonight was meant to show him he had better play ball or else!'

'They thought that I was involved with him?' Eden was so shocked, she could barely force the words out.

'Of course. After all, it's what I believed too.' He gave a short, harsh laugh. 'I wonder if you realised exactly what you were getting yourself into when you agreed to play along with this little game? Deceiving me was one thing, Eden, but I very much doubt you realised you were putting yourself on the line for what happened here tonight, did you?'

'What do you mean? You surely don't believe that I was a party to it...to any of it?' She scrambled unsteadily to her feet, staring at him with shocked eyes, and saw the cold, contemptuous smile he gave with a sinking heart.

'Of course you were. You had ample opportunity to tell me the truth from the moment I turned up on your doorstep. I have to hand it to you, you really are a cool customer all right. You played along beautifully, hardly put a foot wrong. But that could be easily attributed to the experience you've had living a dual life in the past. And, of course, there was the money as an added consideration, I expect. How much did Lewis pay you for your co-operation, Eden? I hope it was generous, considering how much it nearly cost you tonight!'

'Why, you...!' Her hand arced through the air but before it could connect with his cheek he caught her wrist, forcing it down behind her back. In the firelight his face was a furious mask, his eyes burning like molten steel.

'The truth hurts, doesn't it? But I've warned you before about doing that!'

He dragged her to him so fast that the quilt slid from her shoulders to pool around her feet while her bare breasts grazed against the hard wall of his chest. Eden cried out but the sound was swallowed up by his mouth as it took hers in a harsh, burning kiss which was filled with a raw kind of anger and something else, something which stilled her frantic struggles, made her heart pound so fast that she might have been running a race, made the blood swirl through her veins. Anger and this raw, elemental passion was a potent mixture, a heady assault on senses which had already been stretched beyond their limits. What had started out as a bitter denial of allegations which hurt ended up as a spiral of uncontrollable desire which shocked them both into stillness.

Marcus stared down into her face, a nerve ticking in his jaw. 'It's still there, isn't it? It makes no damned difference that I know you for what you are or that you hate my guts—the sparks still ignite when we touch. How do you explain that, Eden?'

She could explain it so simply, with a few words, but they were words he would neither believe nor want to hear from her. The only way they seemed to be able to communicate was through this wild passion they aroused in one another. It would never be enough but it was all she would have to see her through the long, empty days to come.

'Does it need explaining?' she asked softly. 'Does there have to be an answer for everything in your life, Marcus?'

His hands bruised her bare flesh, fingers imprinting on the smooth whiteness of her skin, as he seemed to fight some sort of silent battle. 'I . . . No! Damn you, Eden, but no, I don't care about answers this time!'

His head lowered towards her but she drew back, suddenly afraid. 'You could regret this, Marcus!'

He stopped, his mouth a hair's breadth away from hers, his warm breath sweet on her lips. 'I might. But it's something I'm willing to risk!'

His eyes blazed with desire as they traced the soft lines of her face then fell slowly to the curves of her body. Eden shuddered, feeling his gaze like something tangible as it slid over her skin. When his mouth found hers again passion erupted, engulfed them both as it spun them away on a hot tide of feelings which left no room for doubts or uncertainties any more.

The fire was hot on her back as Marcus lowered her gently to the quilt, cushioning her on its downy folds as he ran his hands down her body, fingers teasing and tormenting nerve-endings to life.

'Marcus . . .!' Her mouth sought his eagerly, her hands running over his chest and shoulders, feeling the hard outline of the muscles under the damp fabric of his shirt, the burning heat of his skin. He eased himself away to strip off his own clothing and toss it aside while she watched him with a hunger in her eyes that she made no attempt to disguise. The firelight played over the strong lines of his powerful body, turning his tanned skin a richer shade of gold and highlighting the perfection of his muscles.

Eden let her eyes feast on him before raising them to his face, the desire she felt clear and unguarded in their violet depths. Marcus gave a hoarse groan then knelt beside her, kissing her while he smoothed his hands down her body from throat to thigh, his fingers exploring the soft curves.

'Beautiful, Eden,' he murmured huskily. 'So beautiful that it almost makes me forget...'

She understood at once, knew this desire he felt wasn't something he *wanted* to feel. He might want her body but he resented the fact. It didn't alter his basic feelings towards her, so was she a fool to lay herself open to yet more pain?

There was a moment when she felt torn by a sudden sharp fear then it faded. It might be a mistake but making love with Marcus was what she wanted now more than anything. The future would be faced later.

She held her arms out to him and drew him down so that his body covered hers while she kissed him with every scrap of love she felt, and felt him respond with a wild urgency which drove all else from her mind. Now there was just her and Marcus and this passion which was too strong to fight, a passion which carried them away to a place where pain and heartache were just memories. She loved him, and now, in actions if not words, might be the only time to show him that.

Marcus was outside when Eden came downstairs. For a few quiet minutes she stood by the window and watched him while she savoured again the memory of the hours they had shared the night before. They had made love in front of the fire and then again upstairs in her bed with an intensity which made her shudder now to recall it.

She had never imagined it could feel like that. Her experience with Geoff hadn't prepared her for that magical world of sensation. Had it been special for Marcus too? Or had making love with her been no different than with any other woman? The thought stole some of the joy from her heart.

He turned suddenly and saw her standing by the window and Eden was filled with a pain so sharp that she almost cried out as she saw the way his face set into a cold mask. When he came inside, she kept her back to him, staring blindly out of the window.

'I hope I didn't disturb you when I got up.'

He sounded so cool and aloof, almost like a stranger, which was ludicrous in the circumstances. This man had held her and kissed her, shared with her an abandoned passion, yet now he spoke to her as though they had met at a vicarage tea party!

Anger rose in her, fed by pain, and she laughed brittly. 'I was awake already. I'm sorry if that's caused you a problem. What were you hoping to do, Marcus—creep off while I was sleeping and save any awkward goodbyes?'

His eyes narrowed with anger. 'I had no intention of going anywhere. Not until I had checked if you were all right.' He skimmed a hard look over her. 'You had a frightening experience last night.'

'You mean those men and almost drowning?' She laughed tauntingly, colour settling into her cheeks. 'But was it any worse than what happened later?' She took a quick step towards him, hurting and wanting to hit back at him for causing this pain. 'I wonder why you made love to me last night, Marcus?'

'Why do you think?' He met her eyes, one brow lifting slightly as he studied her. 'But to turn the question around, why did you let me, Eden?'

'I tend to forget that you're an expert. Questions and countering them is your field!'

'What do you want me to say?' He sighed heavily, as though he found the conversation tedious. 'Do you want me to apologise for what happened?'

'No!' The last thing she wanted was that!

'Then I suppose the simple answer is that the drama of last night affected both of us.'

'Is that right? So how do you explain what happened by the lake at Becky's house?' Why was she pursuing it? Why didn't she just let things be? It was what she should do, of course, yet for some reason she felt a need to break through this icy barrier he had erected.

'Lust.' He laughed harshly when she flinched, her face going white. 'Why pretend, Eden? You're a passionate woman. You arouse desires in a man which are difficult to control. But I'm sure you're well aware of the effect you have on men. And why should I be any different from all the others who've fallen under your spell?'

She didn't think she could stand the agony of hearing what he thought yet even then she couldn't seem to stop. 'So last night hasn't changed how you feel?'

'Should it have?' He went and picked up his jacket and slipped it on, glancing back at her with an arrogant half-smile. 'I deal with facts, not emotions. I look at the evidence and make my judgements accordingly.' One black brow arched. 'If there's anything else you want to tell me which could alter my view then feel free. I imagine I owe you that at least after last night!'

She looked away from his mocking face. She could tell him the truth, of course, all of it. She could explain about Eleanor and how she had wanted to protect her, tell him all about her marriage and those lies in the papers; she could tell him every single thing. But what was the point? For it to mean anything then Marcus should know in his own heart that the woman who had lain in his arms last night and *loved* him couldn't be the person he thought her to be!

'Well, Eden?'

She turned to walk to the kitchen, barely sparing him a glance as she walked past. 'No, thank you. I can't think of anything at all I want to tell you, Marcus, apart from goodbye. I just hope that this will be the end of it. I imagine I have paid my full dues, don't you?'

He caught her arm and spun her round, eyes blazing, jaw set. 'You've paid nothing compared to what this is going to cost Becky! I hope you're proud of your part in all this. You might not have had an affair with Lewis but you're just as guilty as your sister for covering up for her! And that's something I can never forgive you for!'

The door slammed behind him but Eden remained where she was instead of going to the window to watch him leave. She didn't need to see him go to feel the pain of the parting. She loved him, and for a few precious hours last night she had been able to show him that with her body. But she would never be able to tell him in words because it was something he wouldn't want to hear.

CHAPTER ELEVEN

EDEN waited until she got home before opening the letter. She'd known it was from Eleanor as soon as she had seen the handwriting. On her way back from the village she had toyed with the idea of simply ripping it up and throwing it away but somehow she couldn't bring herself to do that. She might want to forget about everything that had happened but Eleanor was her sister and she couldn't turn her back on her no matter how painful it was to think about what had gone on.

She went down to the cove and sat on the sand and stared quietly across the glittering blue waters of the bay then took a slow breath and tore the envelope open to read the single sheet of paper it contained. When she had finished she ran her hand over Drac's silky head as he came and lay down beside her and blinked back a sudden mist of tears.

The letter had been brief but poignant. Eleanor had written to ask Eden to forgive her, if she could, for all she'd done. She would understand if Eden never wanted to see or speak to her again but she'd just wanted to apologise and tell her that she had come to her senses at last and wouldn't be seeing Rob Lewis again. All she could hope now was that Eden wouldn't hate her...

Eden folded the letter and put it carefully back in the envelope with a sad smile. She didn't hate Eleanor; she never would. Hatred was too bitter an emotion to live with. Living with the memory of Marcus's hatred had proved that.

The memory of that last time she had seen him was still so raw that she ached at the thought. It had been two weeks now, two long weeks of unrelenting agony as she relived daily what Marcus had said before he'd left. She loved him... and he hated her; it almost tore her in two to face it.

'Eden... are you all right?'

She started nervously, swinging round to see Shiloh Smith halfway down the path. Drac growled as he shot to his feet and she hooked her hand under his collar to hold him back.

'What do you want?' Her tone was little short of rude but she made no apology for it. Shiloh Smith was part and parcel of what had happened and that hardly endeared him to her!

He gave a rueful smile as he came towards her, stopping when Drac growled a warning. 'I see he hasn't forgiven me.'

At Eden's questioning look he continued, with a wry laugh, 'I locked him in the kitchen that night. That pair would have thought nothing of shooting him if he'd got in the way, but he doesn't appreciate that!'

Eden glanced at the dog, then back at the man. She hadn't seen him since that night. The yacht had disappeared from the bay the following day and she had been too cut up by everything that had happened between her and Marcus to make enquiries. Now, suddenly, she wanted answers!

'You knew what was going on, then?' She laughed bitterly. 'Of course you did! You're one of O'Rourke's men!'

He came and sat beside her, staring out across the bay. 'I was doing my job, Eden. It was essential that we find out who was passing on the information. It was a pity that you got involved.'

'You were here to check up on me, weren't you? To find out what part I had in it all?' She gave a hard little laugh. 'And I wonder how far you were prepared to go to that end! Were you responsible for that break-in? What were you looking for? Evidence of my involvement. I doubt you found any!'

'No.' Shiloh's voice was flat. 'That pair of charmers who turned up that night were behind that. I imagine it was intended as a warning to Lewis that they meant business. However, seeing as you and he weren't involved as everyone thought, it didn't have the desired effect.'

Eden laughed out loud. 'Oh, dear! I did cause everyone a lot of problems! I had you fooled, those men fooled and... and Marcus as well!' Her voice broke on Marcus's name and she looked away as she swallowed down the lump in her throat.

'It wasn't difficult, not when Lewis set out to achieve that objective too.'

'What do you mean? It was Eleanor's idea to use my name to cover up the affair she was having with him.'

'I'm sure it was. However, Lewis wasn't slow to see the advantages once he found out. From what I can gather he told our "friends" that he'd got the original information about Alessi from Marcus via you. It gave him some breathing space when he couldn't come up with anything fresh.'

'What? Are you sure?'

Shiloh laughed grimly. 'Nothing is ever "sure" when you're dealing with guys like Lewis! But we're pretty certain.'

'Then why did those men try to...to harm me? Surely I was of value to them, the so-called link with Marcus?'

'Lewis must have told them eventually that Marcus didn't know where Alessi is now to try and get himself off the hook. It made no difference, of course, just changed the ball-game in that your role altered. You then became the lever to convince Lewis of what would happen if he didn't come up with the goods.'

'It's horrible, unbelievable...like something out of a film! What's happened to those men now?' She turned to Shiloh, eyes huge and questioning, unaware of the picture she made sitting there in the sunlight with her hair streaming down her back.

'They've been quietly returned to their own country where they will eventually face trial for trying to pervert the course of justice.' He looked away, an odd expression on his face as he narrowed his eyes against the glare from the sea.

'But it isn't over, is it?' She sighed. 'How can you bear to get involved in something like this? All I've had is a small taste of your world but that's enough!'

'Somebody has to do the job, Eden. It might be distasteful but it's never easy upholding principles.'

Eden smiled sadly. 'You sound just like Marcus.' She gave a hollow laugh. 'He accused me once of not having any principles!'

Shiloh glanced at her, his face full of compassion. 'You're in love with him, aren't you?'

'Is...is it that obvious?'

'If you've been there yourself...' He shrugged. 'It's one hell of a mess, isn't it, honey? I wish I could have done more but my hands were tied.'

'What do you mean?'

'I had my suspicions all wasn't what it seemed. After you and Marcus left on the night of the break-in I came back to the cottage and searched through the debris and found some photos of you and Lewis. I couldn't put my finger on it but there was something about them which bothered me.'

He must have heard her shocked gasp because he smiled briefly in apology. 'We needed to find out all we could about you and there wasn't a lot of time to do it. I sensed there was something far more sinister behind that break-in than mere vandalism. Then Harry told me about the two *Italians* who'd booked rooms at the inn then disappeared, and it was just too coincidental. I knew there was something brewing but I couldn't warn you and run the risk of scaring them off before we found out what was going on. Then Marcus told us that the woman involved with Lewis was your sister and all hell broke out.'

'Marcus told you?'

'Yes. He'd forced Lewis to tell him what had been going on then realised the implications, that you could be in danger. He contacted Flynn at once. It was because of Marcus that we got here that night and were in position before those men arrived. Although none of us could have guessed how fast things would move.'

'It wasn't your fault. I chose to let Marcus think I was involved with Lewis, and, indirectly, everyone else. Now...' She swallowed down the lump in her throat, forcing a smile although her eyes were glistening with tears. 'Now it's over.'

'I'm sorry, Eden. I wish there was something I could do.' He got up with a sigh. 'However, I'll be leaving soon. I just called round to say goodbye.'

Eden got up too. 'Are you going home, wherever that is?'

'Colorado. I live in the mountains, although recently I've spent very little time there.'

There was a note in his voice which made Eden's heart lurch. 'This is over? You don't think that anything else will happen?'

He shrugged. 'No one can say for certain that the people behind this won't try again. But your involvement is at an end.'

'And Marcus? They don't still believe he has the information they want?' She gripped Shiloh's hand as a sudden fear assailed her. If anything happened to Marcus she couldn't bear it!

'No.' Shiloh squeezed her fingers. 'They're aware that he doesn't know anything. They won't try using him again; rest assured of that.'

Eden shuddered. 'It's a nightmare!'

'But no longer your nightmare, Eden. Your part in this is finished.' Shiloh bent and kissed her cheek then stared quietly into her eyes. 'Marcus is a lucky guy. Just make sure he realises it.'

'I——'

'Get your hands off her, Smith!'

The sound of that deep, angry voice made her sway. Eden would have fallen if Shiloh hadn't steadied her. She glanced round, her heart stopping as she saw Marcus standing by the rocks, his face set into grim lines which boded ill for everyone!

'Marcus, I...'

He ignored her as he strode towards them, his grey eyes glacial as they locked on to the other man. 'I said get your hands off her. Are you hard of hearing or something?'

Shiloh smiled narrowly, glancing down at Eden with a faint gleam of amusement in his eyes which stalled her instinctive attempts to move away from him. '"Or something" could be about right, Cole.' He let his huge hands slide up Eden's arms, lightly stroking her skin as he watched Marcus. 'Give me one good reason why I should let her go. What is it to you anyhow?'

Marcus swore colourfully, his face thunderous, body rigid with tension. 'I'm warning you, Smith. I'm in no mood to play games. Let her go!'

'I imagine that's up to Eden. Don't you agree?' He laughed softly, his eyes holding a warning look as they met Eden's startled ones. 'Do you want me to let you go, honey?'

What was Shiloh playing at? Did he really believe that Marcus was jealous? It was ridiculous, yet when she chanced a look in Marcus's direction and saw the anger on his face, the steely glitter in his scorching gaze, the possibility seemed to set down roots. Her heart leapt at the heady thought because it led on to so many others...!

She sucked in breath as though she were drowning again, and played the role of her life. 'Well, that depends, Shiloh.'

His smile encouraged her. 'Mmm? On what?'

'On the reason why Marcus is acting like the proverbial dog in a manger.' She gave a taunting little laugh, looking past the man who held her to the man who possessed her heart and soul. 'Marcus has made no secret of how he feels about me, so why should it make a scrap of difference if he finds me in your arms or any other man's?'

Marcus met her taunting stare, his face like a mask. 'Why indeed? I should have known, shouldn't I? I should have realised that you wouldn't last long without a man!'

He swung round on his heel but if he thought for a moment that he could get away with that he was mistaken! Eden tore herself away from Shiloh and ran after him to catch hold of his arm. 'Damn you, Marcus Cole! How dare you accuse me of that?'

'Very easily.' He removed her hand from his arm, his mouth curled into a smile which cut her heart to ribbons with its contempt and chilling mockery. 'Do you know why I came here today, my sweet little sinner? I came to find out once and for all if I had been mistaken. But I don't think I need to stop around any longer, do I? I think I've got all the answers I need!'

He carried on walking, ignoring Eden when she called his name, her voice filled with pain and a raw kind of anger. He was walking out on her again and she would never get the chance to make him understand how wrong he was!

Desperation filled her and she looked round helplessly then found the answer, a surefire way to make Marcus stop and listen for as long as she wanted him to!

'Drac, hold!' Her voice rang out clearly and the dog leapt to obey. With a few swift bounds he chased after Marcus and caught hold of his arm, bringing him to a sudden stop.

'What the devil...?' Marcus's face was a picture as he tried to free himself but the dog just growled a warning as he held on to him.

Eden walked the few steps it took to bring her face to face with him. She could be about to make a fool of herself but it was a chance she was going to take! 'I shall tell Drac to let you go only if you promise to stay here and listen to what I have to say.'

'You don't have anything to say that I want to hear! Now stop playing games, Eden. I warn you I'm in no mood for this!' Fury darkened his eyes to almost black, made a nerve beat heavily in his cheek, yet there was just something about the way he was looking at her which made her heart lift, made her think that maybe making a fool of herself was a risk worth taking.

She took another slow step then stopped just inches away from him as she stared quietly into his face. 'Why did you come, Marcus?'

He looked away, face grim and uncompromising, voice harsh when he finally answered. 'Because I was fool enough to imagine that maybe, just *maybe*, I'd been wrong about you!'

'And that makes a difference?' She moved again, so close that their bodies were almost touching. Heat from his skin flowed over her, warming away the chill which seemed to have filled her for these past weeks.

'Of course it makes a difference!'

'Why? I mean, even if you suddenly discovered that you had been completely wrong, why should it alter anything, why should it affect your life in any way at all?'

There was a moment when she didn't think he was going to answer, a moment when her heart broke just that little bit more. Then Marcus spoke, the words ground out from between his tightly clenched jaw. 'Because I love you, damn it! I love you, Eden!'

The joy she felt was so sweet that her head reeled with its effects. Slowly, so slowly that it felt like a dream, she moved the last inch and laid her hands on his chest as she stared into his eyes. 'And I love you too, Marcus.'

So many fleeting emotions crossed his face, from disbelief to anger to a slow acceptance that she was telling the truth. 'Then don't you think it's time we did something about it?' he said harshly.

Eden laughed. 'I think it's way past time!'

Marcus returned her smile, bending to kiss her, only to come to a sudden halt when Drac growled. He raised a mocking brow as he glanced at the dog. 'Do you think you could make him let me go? Otherwise I could find my movements somewhat...restricted.'

Heat flowed along her veins at the note in his voice and she flushed hectically, hearing Marcus's soft laugh as he saw her heightened colour and correctly interpreted its cause.

'Now, where was I?' Marcus moved towards her as the dog released him, then stopped again when Shiloh coughed discreetly.

'I guess I'm in the way so I'll say goodbye. Be happy, both of you.' He sketched them a wave then started up the path. Eden stared after his retreating figure with a faint smile.

'It isn't too late to stop him, Eden.' Marcus's voice was hard but it didn't quite conceal the pain and she turned back to him, seeing behind the cool mask at last.

'But I don't want to stop him. It's you I love, Marcus. Only you. There was never anything between Shiloh and me despite what you thought.'

Marcus grimaced as he reached out and drew her close, holding her as though he would never let her go. 'I've been such a fool, Eden, such a blind, stubborn fool!'

'You have.' She laughed lovingly. 'You don't want me to lie to you, do you, darling?'

He curled his fingers through her hair and tilted her head back, biting gently at the exposed cord in her neck in a sensuous and tormenting punishment. 'I think a small white one might have been permissable in the circumstances, wretch!'

Eden shuddered at the feel of his mouth on her skin. She stared deeply into his eyes, wanting him to understand. 'Not even white ones between us from now on, Marcus. Only the truth.'

He cupped her face with a gentle hand. 'And the truth is that you love me?'

There was a need for reassurance in his voice which made her heart overflow. To find Marcus, strong, tough, uncompromising Marcus, suddenly vulnerable was achingly poignant. 'Yes. I love you. I love you more than I can tell you, probably even more than I can show you, but I shall spend my whole life trying to make you believe it if you'll let me.'

'Eden!' Her name was a raw admission of need which sent a responsive shudder racing through her. When he kissed her with that same need, Eden gave him everything he asked for, wanting only to make him believe how deep her love for him was.

That first wild kiss led to another then whirled into a passion which demanded release. When Marcus drew her down beside him on the sand, she gave herself to him willingly with joy filling her heart. She loved him so, and he loved her. It seemed as though heaven had fallen into her grasp.

'I love you, Eden.' Marcus's voice held a note which brought tears to her eyes as their bodies joined in the ultimate act of love and faith. Eden framed his face, kissing his mouth, his jaw, his eyelids, anywhere and everywhere she could, driving out the last of the pain with her unstinted love.

'I love you too,' she whispered, then repeated it as passion claimed them both and swirled them away on its own wild tide. 'I love you, Marcus!'

The sun was dipping towards the horizon by the time they lay spent and at peace, arms entwined, bodies pressed closely together. Marcus tilted her face up and pressed a lingering kiss on her swollen lips, his eyes tracing the delicate line of her nose and jaw, the purity of her skin.

'You're so beautiful, Eden. I think it was your beauty which scared me from the first moment I saw you.' He gave a rueful sigh, drawing her head into the hollow of his shoulder as he held her to him. 'I knew that if I ever once allowed myself to acknowledge it then I would be putty in your hands!'

Eden laughed softly, nuzzling his neck with tiny open-mouthed kisses, loving the way a shudder ran through his powerful body even now, after the way they had made love with such wild abandonment. 'I never took you to be a coward, Marcus.'

'Neither did I . . . until you appeared and turned my world upside-down. Life had been so simple until then. Then I paid you that visit and it all erupted.' He kissed her hard and swiftly, pain shadowing his eyes. 'I'm sorry about all the things I said to you, all those cruel accusations I made. The only excuse I have is that I was determined Becky wouldn't suffer, but it's not much of an excuse, is it? Not for all my cruelty.'

'You did what you thought best.' She ran her hand down his cheek. 'I never wanted to deceive you, Marcus. It wasn't planned. I had no idea what Eleanor had done or that she'd involved me. When you turned up on the doorstep with those photos I didn't know what to do.

The only clear thought in my head was that I had to protect Eleanor and give her a chance to sort the mess out.' She laughed hollowly. 'I had no idea just what I was getting into!'

'I know. I went to see your sister and made her give me some answers. She'd heard about what had happened to you and I think she was just beginning to realise how things could have turned out. She held nothing back and explained everything to me, the fact that you had no idea what had been going on, that you would have felt it your duty to help her when I turned up.' He hugged Eden to him and held her there, close to his heart. 'I knew at once that it was the truth. It was what I wanted to hear because I'd realised that I'd been wrong about you. I'd just been afraid to admit it to myself because of the implications! But your only crime was being too loyal, Eden, and trying to protect your sister.'

'It's still hard to take in. That Eleanor should have got involved with Lewis in the first place...!' She sighed. 'I don't think she's ever really been the same since the breakdown she had after our parents died. Eleanor was driving the car when it crashed; she'd only just got her licence, and although she was exonerated at the inquest she blamed herself. She's always been emotionally vulnerable and she met Rob Lewis at a time when everything seemed to be going wrong in her life. Thank God she's seen sense now!'

'Finding out about Becky's baby had a lot to do with it.' Marcus smiled grimly. 'Rob had overlooked mentioning it, evidently. When I told Eleanor I think it brought home to her that everything Rob had told her had been a pack of lies for his own ends.'

'What do you mean?'

'Simply that once Rob discovered Eleanor wasn't you he saw the advantages of the situation. I'd been fooled into believing that you and he were involved, so why shouldn't the men who were hounding him for information be fooled as well? It gave him a bit of breathing space while he planned what to do.' Marcus shrugged. 'The only stumbling-block was Eleanor, who was feeling guilty and talking about telling you and me the truth. That was the last thing Rob wanted. I can't prove it but I suspect he made sure that Ben found out about their affair. He knew how devastated Eleanor would be and that it would be much easier to persuade her to do what he wanted if she was dependent upon him for emotional support.'

Eden gasped. 'Is that why he talked her into going away with him?'

'Yes. He was desperate to delay those men from finding out that he'd been lying to them. He didn't give a damn what they might do to you so long as it kept them off his back!' His hands tightened and he held her as though he would never let her go, his whole body shuddering with anguish.

Eden smoothed her hand down his cheek. 'But it didn't work out that way, Marcus, thanks to you.'

'That your life should have been put at risk, though...!' His mouth was hard and hungry, fierce as it took hers in a kiss which showed how he must have suffered, reliving that night since. Eden kissed him back, loving him more than ever, feeling cherished and safe in his arms.

He drew back slowly, cupping her face in his hands. 'No one will ever get the chance to hurt you again, my love, not while there is breath in my body!'

Eden smiled shakily, pressing a soft kiss to his lips.
'I know.' She gave a small laugh, nestling into his arms,
feeling their strength enclosing her. 'But let's not dwell
on it any more. It's over. Eleanor wrote and told me that
she won't be seeing Lewis again.'

'So I believe. She's also going to see her fiancé. I think
there's a chance they'll try again.'

'Oh, I'm so glad! Maybe it hasn't been so bad after
all. We would never have met if none of this had happened.' She smoothed a finger across his mouth then
gasped when he nipped it in a sensual love-bite.

'Then maybe I should try feeling grateful to my soon-
to-be-ex-brother-in-law, only it isn't easy!'

'So Becky found out about everything?'

Marcus nodded, his eyes suddenly bleak. 'There was
no way of keeping it from her. I don't think that she
was as shocked as I might have expected. Becky must
have had an inkling of what was going on and my one
regret is that perhaps I was wrong in trying to protect
her.'

'So what does she intend to do?'

'Divorce Lewis as soon as she can find him.'

Eden drew back. 'You mean he's left the country?'

'Yes. I imagine he thought it was the safest thing to
do.'

'How awful for Becky.'

'It is, of course. But she's bearing up remarkably well
and showing great courage. She intends to have the baby
before making any major decisions about her life,
although I think she's going to have a little help there.'

'What do you mean?'

He gave a faint smile. 'Remember Daniel Faramond
at Natalie's wedding?' When Eden nodded he continued, 'He's been around a lot recently, helping Becky

through it all. He lost her once before but this time I don't think he intends to let that happen again!'

'I'm glad. Becky's so nice I would hate to think of her being sad and lonely, although she must hate me for my part in all this.'

There was regret in her voice and Marcus skimmed his hand up her body and curled it over her shoulder, his fingers smoothing over her skin, setting up a flash-fire of sensation which made her shudder. He smiled with satisfaction and bent to kiss her with devastating thoroughness. 'Becky doesn't hate you. I've explained it all to her and she understands. And now I can think of a dozen more interesting things to do than talk about this fiasco any longer!'

Eden laughed shakily, running her hands over his chest, feeling the heavy throbbing of his heart under her palms. 'I'm sure you can! But...'

'But we need to get it cleared up.' He stared into her eyes, his own gaze so grave that Eden felt her heart skip a beat before he continued. 'I don't want our future together to be tainted by this, my love.'

'Do...do we have a future...together, Marcus?'

'I can't imagine one without you. I don't want to try! I realised that shortly after I walked out that morning.' He closed his eyes as though the thought was unbearable then opened them again, a steely determination in their depths which only made her love him more. No matter what, Marcus would always face things head-on. It was one of the things she loved most about him.

'I never expected to see you again,' she admitted quietly. 'When you left I thought that was the end. It almost broke my heart because I love you so much.'

'And I was too stubborn to admit that I loved you! I kept looking at the so-called evidence and trying not to hear what my heart was telling me, Eden.' He gave a wry laugh. 'Too many years of dealing with the law, but the law isn't much of a guide when it comes to matters of the heart! Everything pointed towards you being what the papers had made you out to be, from that supposed affair to Smith hanging around!'

He made no attempt to hide his annoyance and Eden laughed, amused that that still rankled. 'There was never anything between Shiloh and me although his reasons for being around weren't completely innocent!'

'I'll bet!'

'Now, now, Marcus. I'll get the idea that you're jealous if you carry on like that.'

'I am and I make no apology for it. It was just too coincidental when he turned up that night!'

'He was just trying to find out all he could.' She shrugged. 'Maybe he was watching out for me but not for that reason. In fact he searched the cottage after we left and turned up those photographs of Eleanor and Lewis.'

'I see. I wonder if he found them as puzzling as I did?' At her look of enquiry Marcus continued, with a low laugh, 'There was just something about them... I only wish I'd examined them more closely then maybe this would have been cleared up sooner!'

'Maybe.' Eden looked away, feeling a sudden shaft of pain. 'But if I hadn't lied to you there wouldn't have been a problem. I... I caused everyone an awful lot of trouble and they must all think badly of me even if Becky has forgiven me. I hate the thought of the people you care for, like Natalie and Flynn, hating me. In the end it could ruin our relationship!'

He kissed her softly, eyes tender and loving. 'No one hates you, sweetheart. They all understand that you were more the victim than the perpetrator.'

'But what about...about my past, and Geoff and everything?' She gave a sad little sigh. 'Mud sticks and there was a lot of mud about when he died.'

'It was all lies, Eden!'

She smiled, loving him for his instantaneous defence of her. 'It was but it hurt and it could come back to haunt us in the future. Geoff's death was an accident. The night it happened I'd told him that I was leaving him because I couldn't take his jealousy any longer. He just seemed to lose control. He jumped into his car and drove off at a furious speed, completely missed the bend in the road and crashed into a wall. But he never meant to kill himself, I am certain of that. Suicide was never in his mind but the papers made much of it.' She caught Marcus's hands in hers and held them tightly, afraid to say what she knew she must. 'What would it do to your career if it ever surfaced again? I couldn't bear to think that you would suffer because of me.'

'If it surfaces we shall face it together. The only thing I couldn't bear is not having you in my life, Eden. Nothing else matters!' He drew her into his arms and held her close. 'I love you. I want to spend the rest of my life with you, building a future together. There has never been any woman I've wanted to do that with.'

'Not even Natalie?' She drew back and searched his face. 'I sensed that there was an empathy between you and her at the wedding.'

Marcus laughed deeply, a husky sound which sent shivers racing through her. 'Natalie is a dear friend and that's all she's ever been! Oh, I think that at one point she did have a bit of a crush on me but Flynn O'Rourke's advent into her life put paid to that! It's you I love, my sweet little sinner, you I want to spend my life with.'

Eden pretended to glare at him, loving him more than ever for the frank admission. 'Sinner? Just who do you think you are to call me a sinner, Marcus Cole?'

'The man you are going to marry, sweetheart, that's who.' He tilted her face and stared into her shocked eyes. 'You will marry me, Eden?'

'I... Yes!' She flung her arms around his neck and pulled his head down to kiss him then found herself enveloped in his arms as he kissed her back, love's sweet tide flowing all around them. Saint and sinner... it had definite possibilities!

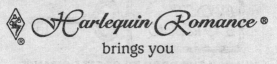
Harlequin Romance ®

brings you

How the West Was Wooed!

We've rounded up twelve of our most popular authors,
and the result is a whole year of romance, Western
style. Every month we'll be bringing you a spirited,
independent woman whose heart is about to be lassoed
by a rugged, handsome, one-hundred-percent cowboy!
Watch for...

• April: **A DANGEROUS MAGIC**—Patricia Wilson

• May: **THE BADLANDS BRIDE**—Rebecca Winters

• June: **RUNAWAY WEDDING**—Ruth Jean Dale

• July: **A RANCH, A RING AND EVERYTHING**—Val Daniels

• August: **TEMPORARY TEXAN**—Heather Allison

BRIDE'S BAY RESORT

UNLOCK THE DOOR TO GREAT ROMANCE AT BRIDE'S BAY RESORT

Join Harlequin's new across-the-lines series, set in an exclusive hotel on an island off the coast of South Carolina.

Seven of your favorite authors will bring you exciting stories about fascinating heroes and heroines discovering love at Bride's Bay Resort.

Look for these fabulous stories coming to a store near you beginning in January 1996.

Harlequin American Romance #613 in January
Matchmaking Baby by Cathy Gillen Thacker

Harlequin Presents #1794 in February
Indiscretions by Robyn Donald

Harlequin Intrigue #362 in March
Love and Lies by Dawn Stewardson

Harlequin Romance #3404 in April
Make Believe Engagement by Day Leclaire

Harlequin Temptation #588 in May
Stranger in the Night by Roseanne Williams

Harlequin Superromance #695 in June
Married to a Stranger by Connie Bennett

Harlequin Historicals #324 in July
Dulcie's Gift by Ruth Langan

Visit Bride's Bay Resort each month wherever Harlequin books are sold.

HARLEQUIN ®

BBAYG

New from Harlequin Romance
a very special six-book series by

The town of Hard Luck, Alaska, needs women!

The O'Halloran brothers, who run a bush-plane service called **Midnight Sons**, are heading a campaign to attract women to Hard Luck. *(Location: north of the Arctic Circle. Population: 150—mostly men!)*

"Debbie Macomber's *Midnight Sons* series is a delightful romantic saga. And each book is a powerful, engaging story in its own right. Unforgettable!"

—Linda Lael Miller

TITLE IN THE MIDNIGHT SONS SERIES:

#3379 BRIDES FOR BROTHERS (available in October 1995)
#3383 THE MARRIAGE RISK (available in November 1995)
#3387 DADDY'S LITTLE HELPER (available in December 1995)
#3395 BECAUSE OF THE BABY (available in February 1996)
#3399 FALLING FOR HIM (available in March 1996)
#3404 ENDING IN MARRIAGE (available in April 1996)

Yo amo novelas con corazón!

Starting this March, Harlequin opens up to a whole new world of readers with two new romance lines in SPANISH!

Harlequin Deseo
- passionate, sensual and exciting stories

Harlequin Bianca
- romances that are fun, fresh and very contemporary

With four titles a month, each line will offer the same wonderfully romantic stories that you've come to love—now available in Spanish.

Look for them at selected retail outlets.

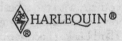